"YOU SON OF A . . . "

A voice reached him from somewhere close to Longarm's back. "You got no business here."

There was no real reason why Longarm should assume that the words were directed toward him. After
all, who the hell did he know in Fairplay these days?

Yet, it was true that the voice sounded vaguely familiar to him.

He frowned.

"Damn you, Long. Are you listening to me, you
son of a . . . "

His frown deepening into a scowl, Longarm turned
around to confront whoever this was who had such a
firm opinion about him.

TABOR EVANS

LONGARM

AND THE LADY FAIRE

J

JOVE BOOKS, NEW YORK

LONGARM AND THE LADY FAIRE

A Jove Book / published by arrangement with
the author

PRINTING HISTORY
Jove edition / October 1997

The Putnam Berkley World Wide Web site address is
http://www.berkley.com

ISBN: 0-515-12162-2

A JOVE BOOK®
Jove Books are published by The Berkley Publishing Group, a
member of Penguin Putnam Inc., 200 Madison Avenue, New York,
New York 10016.
JOVE and the "J" design are trademarks
belonging to Jove Publications, Inc.

PRINTED IN THE UNITED STATES OF AMERICA

10 9 8 7 6 5 4 3 2 1

Chapter 1

Longarm checked the list carefully, verified that this was indeed the address he wanted, then just as carefully folded the sheet of paper and replaced it in the inside pocket of his tweed coat. He yawned once—it had been a long day—and mounted the steps of the boardinghouse.

When the landlady responded to his knock, Longarm was wearing a look of amiable greeting. Despite his height, something in excess of six feet, and his rugged build, he managed to appear mildly inoffensive and perhaps even a trifle simple.

"Ma'am." He smiled and dipped his head so as to more easily touch the brim of his flat-crowned, snuff-brown Stetson hat.

"If you're selling something, mister . . ."

"No, ma'am, not me. I'm here to see a fellow I'm told is one of your boarders. John David Howard? I was told I might find him at dinner about now?"

The landlady—her features looked to be about as hard

as a Number Three drill bit—scowled and demanded, "And what would this visit be that I should bother the gentleman while he's eating?"

"I don't mean t' be a bother, ma'am, but I got a job t' do here. I just need to deliver a paper to the gentleman. Then I'll be on my way again."

"What sort of paper?" the middle-aged harpy wanted to know.

"Subpoena, ma'am. Official business, y' see." Longarm displayed both a badge proclaiming him to be a deputy United States marshal and the official document in question, signed and certified by a federal judge of the First District Court of Colorado in Denver.

He smiled again. Nicely.

"I won't keep the gentleman but a moment. Then he can get back t' what I'm told is the best food t' be found anywhere in or near Fairplay."

The old bat did not rise to his bait. The flattery seemed to do no good whatsoever. Still and all . . .

"Wait here. I will tell Mr. Howard that you want to see him."

"Yes, ma'am. Thank you, ma'am." While Longarm was still talking and again touching the brim of his hat to the old battle-ax, she shut the door on him.

Moreover, he heard the bolt slide closed. He was not going to enter without her say-so, by gum, for after all, a subpoena was no search warrant and Deputy Marshal Custis Long had no more right to the inside of her house than a passing billygoat would.

Oh, well.

Perhaps forty seconds later the back door of the boardinghouse swung open and a lean, dark little man stepped outside. The slightly built fellow was engaged in tugging a cloth cap low over his eyes even as he made his escape across the back stoop.

He appeared ordinary enough save for one disconcerting departure from normal street attire, that being a napkin tucked inside his shirt collar and forgotten in the heat of flight.

2

Longarm did not mind.

He cleared his throat. Loudly. And the small man jumped half out of his skin before whirling about, his eyes going wide at the sight of the tall, undeniably handsome deputy who stood at the edge of the landlady's withering tomato plot. Of course it was probably not the sight of Longarm that captured the man's attention so much as it was the implied threat of the rather large blue-steel Colt revolver that rode in a slanted cross-draw rig on Longarm's belly. If the little man was armed, he was carrying his gun very thoroughly concealed.

"You, uh . . ."

"Evenin', Mr. Howard." Longarm smiled and once more touched the brim of his Stetson. "Fine time o' day for a stroll, isn't it."

"I, um . . ."

"No need for me t' keep you, sir." Longarm held the subpoena out to him, and reluctantly the smallish fellow took it. "The time and place for you to appear is all written down there for you. D' you need directions t' the federal courthouse in Denver? No? I kinda thought maybe not." Longarm turned as if to leave, then reconsidered and turned back again. "I almost forgot t' tell you. Sorry. When you come down, Mr. Howard, get receipts for the train tickets and your meals. You'll be reimbursed for your travel costs. They'll tell you how t' find the clerk an' file for your expenses when you get there."

Mr. Howard looked like he was close to tears. Whatever his testimony was to be—and the truth was that Longarm had no information about that whatsoever; the batch of subpoenas he'd been given were all just so much paper so far as he was concerned—it was a chat that Mr. Howard really did not want to have.

"It'd be a convenience for both of us, sir," Longarm reminded him, "if you come down when it says there." He smiled. In a calm and rather gentle tone of voice he added, "Save me from having t' come up here again an' tote you down in manacles an' leg irons, y' see."

3

Longarm touched the brim of his hat one last time and, still smiling, turned away.

Two more, he thought as he first sniffed, and then took a small, tentative taste of the rye whiskey he'd been served. He frowned just a little. The rye was only so-so. Of course fair-to-middlin' rye was five times better than most whiskeys. But still and all, it was only so-so as far as rye was concerned. Pity.

Two more subpoenas to hand out here in Fairplay, then one in Alma, and from there he could take a coach across Mosquito Pass, jumping from the Platte River headwaters over to the high beginnings of the Arkansas. Both of those major drainages began their existence within a few miles of each other in the mountains of central Colorado. On the Arkansas River side, Longarm had a few more papers to serve in Leadville.

And from there he could head back home to Denver and see what sort of assignment U.S. Marshal William Vail had in store for him next.

Something more interesting than paper hanging, he hoped.

Not that he was complaining. He was not. Serving subpoenas was part and parcel of the business of being a deputy.

And besides, he reminded himself as he took another small bite out of the rye, as long as he was out of town on official business, his expenses were being paid by the Justice Department. And thinking about that did seem to improve the flavor of the whiskey somewhat. So much so that he finished that one and motioned for another.

"You son of a bitch." A voice reached him from a point somewhere close to Longarm's back. "You got no business here."

There was no real reason why Longarm should assume that the words were directed toward him. After all, who the hell did he know in Fairplay these days?

Yet it was true that the voice sounded vaguely familiar to him.

He frowned.

"Damn you, Long. Are you listening to me, you son of a bitch?"

Well, shit, he thought silently to himself.

His frown deepening into a scowl, Longarm turned around to confront whoever it was who had such a firm opinion about him.

Chapter 2

"Up yours, Ed. Sideways." Longarm accepted the whiskey glass the bartender set before him and paid for it, ignoring the fuming, red-faced man who continued to sullenly stare at Longarm's back.

The man, a thin and normally pale fellow with lank blond hair and a brass town marshal's shield—a cheap one, no town name specified, the engraving simply reading "Marshal"—pinned to his vest, came around the table to stand in the line of Longarm's vision.

"I mean it, Long. This is my town, and I want you out of it."

"I'm impressed, Ed. I thought you'd put your tail between your legs and slunk off to wherever you call home. But then I should've known better, I suppose. Hell, they wouldn't want you there either. Likely they know you too well t' want you back."

"I'm the law in Fairplay, Long. Damn you. And don't you forget it."

6

"What you are, Kramer, is a piece of shit. That's what I remember best about you." Longarm took a sip of the whiskey, and wished they stocked just a little better grade of rye there.

Marshal Ed Kramer opened his mouth as if to say something, then apparently thought better of it. He glanced around to see if anyone was paying attention to this exchange between peace officers—no one seemed to be—and without invitation helped himself to a seat immediately in front of Longarm. When he spoke again, his voice was considerably softer than it had been before. "I don't want you here, Long. I don't like you. I didn't like you before Darwin and I like you even less now. You don't have jurisdiction here, dammit, unless I ask for your help, and you know damn good and well I'd rather turn myself over to the Apache for a slow killing than ask any favors from you. So get out of here before I send a wire to your boss and see just how much trouble I can cause you."

Longarm took his time about answering, helping himself first to another sip of rye and then to a carefully trimmed and slowly lighted cheroot before speaking. "You want my boss's name and address, Ed? It's still Billy Vail. Same place as before. An' Billy will remember you about as good as I do, so you tell him anything you want an' see how far it gets you. As for my business here, that's a federal affair. Fairplay is still, so far as I know, a part o' the Ewe-nited States. Which means I can see t' my knitting, whatever it happens t' be, any time I want. But tell me, Ed. Why are you so set against having a federal deputy around? You doing something here like you were down in Darwin? Huh? You want me t' look into your affairs again, partner?"

Two, closer to three, years it had been since Darwin, Longarm realized when he thought about it. That was down in New Mexico Territory. Darwin was—or had been, it had likely disappeared by now—a mining camp in the mountains north of Mora. The place hadn't been much bigger than a pimple on a fat whore's ass, but it had been raw and rugged and full of fight.

Ed Kramer had been town marshal there too. Charged

with the responsibility, among other things, of arranging security for the shipment of gold processed at the community stamp mill and crudely refined there as well so as to avoid having to ship bulky concentrates over the narrow trails leading into the camp. No railroads, not even decent wagon roads, reached Darwin and none ever were likely to.

Avaricious thieves, swarms of them, preyed upon the gold shipments despite Marshal Kramer's last-minute changes of route or plan, despite all the sleight of hand and subterfuge the man devised. The thieves made their business seem downright easy.

Which became somewhat more understandable after a deputy U.S. marshal, a certain Custis Long by name, stepped into the investigation and learned that the thieves were buying information about the gold shipments from Darwin's own Marshal Kramer.

No proof was ever established about that, thanks to the ringleader of the thieves making the fatal mistake of trying to drygulch Longarm and thereby rendering himself unfit for testimony in a court of law, but the townspeople did not need the same degree of proof that a judge might have demanded. Ed Kramer was fired, beaten within an inch of his life, and unceremoniously thrown out of town—literally thrown through the air into a mud pit.

Longarm had not seen the man, nor particularly thought about him, since that time.

He pondered the question now and decided that, no, this meeting was not a pleasure. Not a lick more than the last one had been.

"Up to your old tricks again, Kramer? Are there any unsolved robberies I should look into around Fairplay?"

Kramer looked fit to explode. His ears burned a bright shade of red and his neck turned the color of an overripe beet. "You bastard," he hissed.

"You never were real smart, Ed, so let me tell you what you can't seem t' figure out for your own self. Leave me be. I'm here t' get a job done. And before you go blowing hot again, I'm telling you straight out that I have proper jurisdiction for that job. When it's done, I'll leave. Not

8

before then. An' the truth, Ed, is that if you keep thumping your chest an' challenging me, I just may up an' decide to stay here an' torment you for a while. Maybe even look t' see can I extend that question o' jurisdiction and take an active hand in law enforcement here around Fairplay. Just like I done before down in Darwin. Remember?''

Kramer's miserable expression showed that he remembered Darwin just fine.

There had been a question about jurisdiction then too. Until the thieves made the mistake of stealing a sack containing property of the United States Post Office along with the gold.

That little misjudgment had caused the theft to fall under federal jurisdiction.

Of course Kramer might still have unanswered questions about just exactly how and why a packet of letters, three of them by actual count, happened to find their way into a locked strongbox containing smelted gold ingots. With the principals in the case all dead and buried, there was no reason for the matter ever to come to trial, and therefore there was no need for public disclosure about that serendipitous coincidence.

Had he ever been asked—under oath and under protest— Deputy Marshal Custis Long might have been able to provide some answers.

But of course he had not been asked, and had felt compelled to volunteer any pertinent information only to Billy Vail. He'd certainly never considered discussing the jurisdiction matter with Ed Kramer. And he was not inclined to do so now either. Instead he merely finished his rye and leaned back away from the table a few inches.

''So tell me, Ed. Are you gonna shut your mouth and slink outa here like the dog you are? Or are you gonna pretend t' be a man and reach for that—what is that plow-handled thing you're carrying, a Smith? So hell, Ed, are you gonna shut up or try an' take me face on?''

Longarm was not worried about that invitation. He doubted that Ed Kramer had the balls to try to shoot him in the back, much less eye to eye.

"You have no jurisdiction here, Long. Remember that because I damn sure will, and my town council will jump all over you if you try to interfere in local matters."

Longarm smiled and shook his head. "Ed, you almost give me faith in human nature. You know? I look at you an' see that things don't change. That makes me feel real bad until I recall that most folks are kind an' decent an' fine . . . which is something you'll never your whole life be able t' understand, but it pleases me when you bring it back to mind. G'wan now. Leave me alone so I won't get my hackles up an' feel like I gotta stay here in Fairplay longer than I ought to just on general principles."

"You have until noon tomorrow to finish your business here and get outside the town limits," Kramer said, his voice rising in volume so that others nearby could listen in on his bluster if they were so inclined.

Longarm didn't much give a shit. Kramer was just trying to make a show to convince himself—no one else was apt to believe it anyway—that he was man enough to handle an adversary like Custis Long.

Longarm gave thought to more important business than Ed Kramer and decided that, yes, he would have one more shot of that rye after all, thank you. He motioned to the bartender and dug into a pocket in search of a coin to pay with.

Chapter 3

Longarm laid his napkin beside his plate and leaned back, just about as content as content could be. His belly was full, he'd had a good night's sleep, and in another few days he would be done serving papers and could head home to Denver. There was a certain lady there that he would like to see again. Soon.

No point in getting worked up from thinking about her, though. Better to get this job behind him and then call on the individual in question. Looking—and for that matter touching—was a helluva lot more interesting than merely thinking about her.

Longarm scrawled a signature onto the bottom of the bill the waiter brought to him. After all, the cost of breakfast could as easily go on the government voucher as out of Longarm's pocket. Then he took his time about trimming, warming, and lighting one of his favorite cheroots. The smoke tasted exceptionally fine atop such a good meal. Longarm was in excellent humor as he stepped out onto the sidewalk from the Fairplay Hotel, a three-story affair with all the most modern conveniences, including water from a spring-pipe constantly running in the lavatory. He had already inquired about the address of the next man he was to subpoena, and expected to find the fellow at work at this early hour of the day. That would be . . . he checked the note he'd made to himself . . . in the business district two blocks over and one to the left. Hutton's Mercantile, Bernard Hutton, Proprietor. The witness was not Hutton himself, but the merchant's son, Charles. Or so Longarm was told. He . . .

"Excuse me!" Longarm apologized as, woolgathering, he bumped smack into the shoulder of a lady walking past on the narrow sidewalk.

He stopped, snatched his hat off, and bobbed his head in embarrassment.

Embarrassment, however, changed quickly to astonishment, and Longarm's jaw dropped open wide enough to catch flies.

"Janet? Janet Brennan? I mean . . . I'm sorry. You can't be. Of course you can't be. But for a moment there . . ." Longarm was stammering and twisting the brim of his hat in both hands. "I . . . I didn't mean to . . . you know."

The woman looked at him as if this rude stranger were a bug that needed stepping on.

And then her mouth gaped too and one gloved hand flew to cover it.

"Custis? Custis *Long*! I can't believe it. I . . ."

"Janet. Jesus, it is you."

"What are you doing here?" Both voices blurted out the question as precisely together as if they'd practiced the timing for days.

"I can't believe . . ."

"But where did you . . ."

Both began to laugh then.

And then, as suddenly, both turned quiet and solemn. Longarm could not claim to know what Janet was thinking. But he knew his own reaction was one of embarrassment born of memory. For this was the girl he'd once pledged himself to, once promised faithfully to return to when the fighting was done.

He had not seen her since that long-ago day.

Nor had he made any attempt to.

"Christ, Janet, I . . . I . . . " He did not know what in hell to say next.

"It's all right, Custis. Really." She smiled at him and reached out to capture his hand in hers. The look she gave him was one of friendship, not censure, and Longarm felt a flood of vast relief when she repeated the smile—God, she was still the finest-looking girl, woman, he'd ever in his whole life seen—and then squeezed his hand with genuine warmth and welcome.

"Can I . . . would you have a cup of coffee with me? Or tea? Something?"

The lady—she was elegantly dressed, her clothing and one small but exquisite cameo brooch speaking with the understatement of wealth—paused for a moment as if to consider the time.

Then, the smile returning, she nodded. "Yes, Custis, let's. We have a lot of catching up to do."

Chapter 4

Janet Brennan was still the prettiest girl—all right, at this age maybe she was entitled to being considered a woman, not a girl, but either way, she was still just about the prettiest female creature ever to come down the pike.

It had been . . . what? He had to think back and try to count. Eighteen years? Something like that. Incredible.

And why *hadn't* he gone back? At least to see her. To talk to her. To . . . All right, so the real reason he hadn't returned was clear if he really wanted to be honest about it. He'd been crazy in love with Janet then. Hell, in a way perhaps he still was. But the blunt truth was that Janet had wanted marriage and stability and all that, and Custis Long—that was a very long time before the nickname Longarm was ever applied to him—Custis Long back then hadn't been ready for marriage. Not even to Janet.

It wasn't that he was afraid of responsibility. Hardly that. He'd embraced responsibility in one form or another virtually his whole life long.

14

No, now that he faced up to it—and hadn't it been a helluva while since he'd thought about Janet or home or the past or all the things that might have been—now that he gave some serious thought to the subject, he realized that what he really could not stomach going back to was the idea of farming.

God, he hated plowing. Straining and sweating from can't-see to can't-see. Bust a man's back and bust his heart and all of it for next to nothing. Or less. Lessons hard learned as a kid had taught young Custis that: There is nothing that can wear a man down so thoroughly and so relentlessly as a hardscrabble farm.

Rotting seed and moldy fodder. Rain so little the seedlings would wither and die. Rain so much the tender shoots would drown and die. Sun so hot it would fry a man's brain. Nights so cold they would stunt a plant's growth.

Mules too cantankerous to work. Horses lame more often than not. Cows too gaunt and poor to give milk. Sheep in search of an excuse to die. Goats in search of a way to escape. Hogs looking for something to destroy so that a man had to use himself up trying to fix whatever they managed to ruin.

Farming was for men with faith and patience. And Custis Long had been gifted with neither of those virtues.

No, he hadn't simply failed to return to the girl he left behind. He'd damn well refused to go back and give himself over to the travails of farming.

So how the hell did he explain that to Janet now after all these long years?

He hadn't any idea. Not one.

He swept his Stetson off and as gallantly and grandly as ever he knew how, opened the door for her to pass through.

Janet obviously knew her way around. She nodded brusquely to the young man at the desk in the Fairplay Hotel as she passed serenely through the lobby and straight back to the dining room.

The head waiter, who hadn't bothered to give Longarm so much as a nod earlier, came hustling over with a big smile of welcome to lead the lady and gentleman to a choice table beside the window, well away from the scents and early morning sounds coming from the hotel bar in a separate room across the way to the left.

"Madame," the man said, bowing low and holding Janet's chair with a flourish. "Will you have the usual?"

"Please."

"Sir." The head waiter bowed again, this time to Longarm, and damned if the fellow didn't hold *his* chair too.

Longarm let the man seat him—felt strange, it did—and said, "I'll have coffee, I reckon."

"Yes, sir. Thank you, sir. Thank you." And the fellow bowed for the third time and backed away, still hunched over as if he was having back spasms or something. Longarm managed to keep from laughing out loud. But he thought about it.

"Now," Janet said, her voice perhaps a trifle too bright and brittle, "where were we?"

"You mean, about now?" Longarm asked. "Or . . . you know."

"You look good, Custis."

"So d' you, Janet. I, uh, it occurs t' me that I don't know what your name is these days. Not Brennan any longer, I'd expect."

"No, it is Faire now." She smiled as if holding back an urge to laugh. "With an E."

"Faire with an E on the end?" Longarm thought back for a moment. "Nobody I'd recall then."

"Actually, I believe you would. I waited as long as I reasonably could, Custis. Then I accepted Harrison Faire's proposal."

"Hairy Harry the Fairy?" Longarm blurted out before he had time to think and to clamp his jaw over that initial reaction. He should have. He would have. Except he'd spoken before he thought. The words had leapt out of his mouth and it was too damn late to call them back again.

Janet blushed, but held his gaze with a level look of her own.

"I . . . Christ, Janet, I'm sorry. I shouldn't of said . . ."

"You don't have to apologize, Custis. I understand."

16

"But Jesus, Janet. Harry Faire?"

She shrugged. Then smiled again.

"I never would of . . . "

"It has been a good marriage, Custis."

"He's good t' you?"

"Very."

"You're happy?"

"Yes, of course. And you?"

"Fine. Just fine."

"Tell me about yourself, Custis."

And so he did. A little. He went light on some parts and made light of others. And in truth there wasn't really all that much to tell. Not, anyway, to a lady he'd once been deep in love with.

As for the rest of it, well, a few facts were all that were needed.

"Now what about you, Janet Faire-with-an-E? Tell me about yourself."

"Certainly nothing so exciting as being a deputy United States marshal, Custis. Excuse me. Do you prefer Longarm? I believe you said that is what everyone calls you nowadays."

"From you, Janet, I think I like the old name best." He wanted to reach over and touch her wrist, but knew he shouldn't. And not only because the others in the hotel dining room would be watching. Mostly he knew he had to avoid touching her because the slightest contact with that beloved flesh—God, had they ever been that young and that much in love?—might set off feelings that were better left buried in the past.

Janet took a sip of the tea she'd been served and gave him a smile. Longarm's coffee was untasted and growing cold before him. Not that he was overmuch concerned with coffee at the moment. There were other things of more interest to think about here. "You were gonna tell me about yourself," he prompted.

"Yes, of course. Not that there is so much to tell. You remember Harry. Not the most rugged of men, it is true,

17

but he has a good mind. And Harry is ambitious. Did you know that about him?''

"No," Longarm confessed, "I reckon I never saw that in him." This time Longarm had sense enough to keep his mouth shut about the things he had known—or along with all the others *thought* he'd known—about Harry Faire in that dim and distant past. After all, all youngsters are fairly stupid. Young Custis Long hadn't been exempt from that trait. He and all the other boys could have been, in fact must have been, dead wrong about Harrison Faire back then.

But Jesus, who would have thought . . .

"Yes, Harry is quite ambitious. And clever. He accepted a position—a very minor one to start—at a bank in Cincinnati. He did well there, of course, and learned about banking. Then we moved to Cleveland to a better situation. Then two years ago, when Harry thought we had enough put by, we came here to Fairplay and Harry opened his own bank, the Charter Bank of Fairplay. And there you have it.''

"Which tells me about Harry. What about you, Janet?" Longarm asked.

"Oh, there isn't really anything to say about me. But I do have a daughter. A beautiful girl, Custis. We named her Elaine. You would love her. I know you would."

"Yes, I'm sure I would, Janet. Any child o' yours must be special. How old is she?"

"Seventeen," Janet said, quickly adding, "Is your coffee cold? This tea is atrocious." She scowled and looked around, and the head waiter materialized beside her as if he'd popped into being out of thin air, he was that quick to respond.

Janet complained about her tea in a softly scolding voice, and the waiter acted as if he'd been sentenced to public flogging. And from the man's expression, Longarm suspected some poor *peon* in the kitchen would lose his job over this.

"Please accept my apologies, Mrs. Faire. It will *not* happen again, I assure you."

"All right, Walter, thank you." Janet gave Walter a

scorching look of dismissal, and the fellow practically dragged his nose along the floor as he bowed himself backward and away to find a suitably hot replacement for the cooling tea.

"Maybe I can meet your daughter sometime," Longarm said once Walter had scurried out of sight.

"I would like that," Janet said. Longarm's impression was that she said that politely enough, but that she didn't really very much want him to become acquainted with her family.

And, of course, neither one of them suggested that dear old Custis become reacquainted with Hairy Harry.

But oh, Longarm would have damn sure liked to become closely reacquainted with Janet.

She really was just as pretty now as she'd been the last time he'd seen her.

He wondered now what it would have been like if he had come back to her when the fighting was over and done with. There wasn't any law that said a man had to farm just because he was young and married and had no prospects. Hell, Hairy Harry hadn't gone into farming after he married the prettiest girl in the whole damned valley. And if ever there was a man who had even fewer prospects than Custis Long back then, it would have to have been Harrison Faire.

If he'd gone back . . .

Longarm shivered and shook himself out of that line of thinking. He took up his cup and swallowed down a slug of oily and bitter room-temperature coffee.

It occurred to him to wonder how the head waiter would react if Longarm complained about the coffee being cold after letting it sit untouched for twenty or thirty minutes. Likely dump it over his head. Or worse. Janet, however, now had a cup of steaming fresh tea to sip at.

But then neither Longarm nor any of his kin owned a bank here in town. Could that have anything to do with the difference?

"So tell me more about your daughter," Longarm suggested, grateful that the subject of his non-return hadn't arisen in the conversation.

Apparently Janet did not want to open that topic any more than Longarm did.

Thank goodness.

Longarm smiled and leaned forward and tried to pay attention to what Janet was saying about her kid, trying at the same time to avoid the temptation of peering into the front of Janet's bodice, where a small gap between buttons exposed a little less than a square inch of soft, pale flesh, flesh that Longarm could recall now with startling clarity. And with a most unexpected rush of arousal.

He felt his trousers bulge at the memories that came flooding back to him now.

She'd been so young and fresh, her skin taut and smooth and creamy, delightful to touch. He could remember the shapes, the textures, the flavors her young body gave to him. Could remember to an almost painful degree every last sense and pleasure.

Had the two of them ever really been so young and so much in love?

So much. He had learned so very much from Janet.

And she from him as well, for she'd been a virgin that afternoon when she'd first presented him with the precious gift of herself.

Janet had been a virgin, and Custis had not been very far from it, although at the time he'd thought himself quite the rake and swordsman.

God, they really had been young, hadn't they?

Longarm forced his eyes away from that tiny array of flesh and back into the present, and tried, really and truly did try, to pay attention to what Janet was saying about this child that she'd borne to Harrison Faire-with-an-E.

But it was not easy.

Not even after eighteen years or however the hell long it had been.

It really was not easy.

Chapter 5

Longarm's mood was . . . strange. Running into Janet after all those years was what caused it, he supposed. He kept feeling . . . what? Regret? Surely not. He'd done the right thing in not going back. Hadn't he?

The thought of plodding along behind a mule's skinny ass for all his days, wrestling with the handles of a plow, chopping weeds with a hoe, breaking his back picking peas, swinging a scythe until his arms burned with pain, standing in the sun while fresh dirt and old sweat mingled into an itchy scratchy paste beneath his clothing—all these things and more were repugnant to him.

And all these things and more would have been his eternal fate had he gone back to West Virginia and married Janet those long years past.

And yet . . .

And yet he could still recall with perfect clarity the feel of her skin and the taste of her mouth.

Oh, she had been something else back then. Just a kid, of course. But then he'd been a kid too.

Custis had been a tall, skinny, gangly boy not fully muscled, with no notion of the abilities that would become his.

Janet was demure and shy, with a complexion like fresh cream and eyelashes like dark curly fans.

They were so much in love that it hurt. He wanted her so badly that Longarm—Custis—quite literally hurt. His balls ached and throbbed from the wanting, and sometimes in the long and lonely nights he would fantasize about having Janet naked at his side, and sometimes on those nights his erections would explode so that he would have to creep outside in the darkness to wash away the sticky, humiliating residues that, having burst, nonetheless failed to give him the relief he sought.

She wanted him too. He could feel that in the passion of her kisses, kisses stolen in shadows when no one else was looking, kisses so deep and soulful they attempted to draw each other's very being into their mouths and thus into their trembling bodies.

Longarm could still remember the first time he touched Janet's breast.

It was in her father's corncrib. She'd been sent there to fetch a basket of hard corn for the old spotted sow that was bellied up heavy with a litter of soon-to-be-born pigs.

Custis had come by on the pretext of needing to borrow some twine so he could mend something—he no longer remembered what. He'd gotten his twine and pretended to leave, then overheard Janet telling her mother she would go get the corn for the sow. He slipped around behind the chicken coop and into the crib, where they would be out of sight from the house, where her mother and sisters were, and from the barn, where her father was working.

She had known he would be there. Of course she had. And she came into his arms as sweetly and as naturally as if she belonged there and no place else.

She raised her face to his and kissed him long and deep, her breathing becoming swift and ragged as rapidly as his did, and he knew that Janet was as fiercely eager as he, and so Custis felt bold enough to slide his hand inside her shirt.

There was not space enough between the buttons for his large hand to fit, and so Janet, sweet virgin Janet, unfastened one of the buttons for him, and then he was able to reach inside.

The flesh of her young breast was firm and cool to the touch. She was not large. Barely more than a mouthful. But her nipple was rigid, a hard pink raisin set atop a tiny mound of rubbery flesh, and the feel of her brought Custis to sudden arousal.

Janet was pressed tight against him, and had to feel the bulge at his crotch, but she did not try to move away from it, merely pretended to know nothing about it as she continued to cling to him, her belly soft and warm against the prodding, pulsing thing that was trapped between them.

Her kiss deepened and her face became flushed, and Custis squeezed her breast and kneaded it between fingers made rough from the hard work of the farming. He pinched the hard button that was her nipple and twisted and teased it.

He hurt her. He was sure of that now, but at the time that had been the farthest thing from his mind. Had he known then that he was hurting her, he would have been mortified beyond excuse. And perhaps Janet knew this, and that was why she never let on to him that his crude groping was surely painful to her. She continued to smother him with loving kisses while he squeezed and twisted and pawed at the elegant softness of her breast.

They might have done even more, there in broad daylight with both her parents only footsteps away, for Custis was already thinking to lift Janet's skirt and explore even further, but they heard her father begin to cough as he stepped outside the barn to light his pipe, and quickly, panting with desire and flushed red with the shared excitement of youthfully innocent lust, they stepped rapidly apart.

They stood for a moment, silent, looking into one another's eyes, and without a word Custis whirled and ran out of the crib and down through the orchard toward the road beyond.

Out of sight but not out of mind. To this day he had not

forgotten the silken feel of Janet's breast that long-ago day in West-by-God Virginia.

Nor had he yet forgotten another occasion even more special to him.

Janet hadn't been the first girl Custis had lain with. Although he wished afterward that he'd known to save himself for her. He told himself, almost made himself believe, that if he'd known Janet was yet to come into his life, he would have resisted all earlier temptations—not that they had been so very many, really—and waited so that she would be the first for him just as he was the first boy ever to lie with her.

That day, that night—so long ago it had been; they'd been so terribly young, so innocent and clumsy—they'd been to church. A Sunday afternoon revival service that started with a picnic dinner set out on trestle tables outdoors, and continued within a brush arbor right through until dusk, when another picnic was laid out and served.

Longarm—Custis—remembered not a word from all the sermonizing that interminably long day. The only reason he'd consented to stay was because Janet was there and by seating himself in the row behind her and a few places to the side he could spend those hours looking at her and fantasizing about her without anyone knowing. He gazed quite literally for several hours at the delicate shape of her ear and the tender curve of her neck and jaw.

He remembered even now the way her hair curled, and the errant wisp of it that escaped to bounce and dangle with every tiny movement of her pretty head.

And then dark was coming and the congregation took a break in the singing and the preaching. Lamps and lanterns were lighted around the grove, and baskets and bundles of foods were opened and spread out for all to share from.

The people drifted, chattering and weary, toward the food. Except for Janet. She went onto tiptoes to whisper something to her mother. Then, laughing, she ran outside the circle of pale light.

Custis followed. She'd known he would. He was positive about that. She was waiting for him among the trees, hidden there until he came near, and then she stepped out, smiling, to show herself to him.

"This way." She took him by the hand and led him through the grove and beyond a thicket of brambles to a tiny glade where the grass was deep and the earth moist and smelling richly of loam.

"Shh," she warned as she covered his mouth with hers. "No one else knows about this place. Don't make no noise, Custis. Don't call nobody else in."

They kissed, and once again he felt her breasts, both of them this time, and once again Janet helped by unbuttoning her blouse so he could more easily gain access to the delights of her flesh.

He groaned and kissed her deeper yet and tugged, pulling her down with him to their knees, and then, his arm in the small of her back to ease her down gently, onto the ground, so that the two young people were for the first time lying side by side.

He felt her, groping and grabbing her, and was encouraged to realize that Janet was feeling him too now, her hands ranging over his face and neck, down onto his chest and lower belly.

And then—he could scarcely believe it—she was actually fondling the mound of desire at his crotch. She touched it without him having to ask it of her, and Custis damn near squirted into his drawers. It was probably the surprise of it that kept him from doing so, because the slightest touch should have been enough to set him off like a keg of French powder exposed to a lighted match.

Janet touched him, and Custis gasped and squeezed her breast all the harder.

He dropped his hand to her thigh, swept the hem of her skirt high, and felt of the warmth of her leg. The softness of her belly.

And then, incredibly, the wet, furry softness of Janet's pussy.

She moaned aloud and lifted her hips to meet his clumsy touch, and Custis knew that this time they had gone too far to stop. This time . . .

He knelt over her and bunched her skirt around her waist, and began tugging and struggling with the ruffled obscenity that was in his way.

"Don't," she whispered, her voice urgent. "Wait, dear."

"But I . . ."

"You'll tear it if you keep on grabbing at it like that, Custis, and then my mother will know for sure what's goin' on a'twixt us."

"But . . ."

"Shh. Leave be, honey. Let me get 'em off for you, Custis dear."

That was better. That was all right. He settled back a mite, and Janet skinned out of her bloomers and smiling, opened herself to him.

There was a sliver of moon high in the sky. He wished it was daylight so he could see her better. But he could see enough. God, she was beautiful. Her belly was pale and the hair at her crotch soft and curly and beaded with tiny pearls of the wetness that her excitement caused.

Janet sat up and leaned forward. She kissed him briefly, and then concentrated on unfastening the buttons at his fly. She seemed very matter-of-fact about what she was doing. But then all the decisions had been made before now. Now she was concentrating on giving this great gift to the boy she loved.

"There," she said with satisfaction as the last button came free and she pushed Custis's britches and drawers down past his hips.

"Oh, honey," she whispered. "It's so pretty."

Custis felt a rush of pleasure at the compliment. And relief that she was not shocked. But then Janet was a farm girl. She'd seen animals couple her whole life long. The mechanics of sex were familiar to her, and the thought of screwing held no terror for her.

She touched him, a light and gentle pass of her fingertips over his engorged flesh, and he trembled. His cock bobbed with each heartbeat and jumped almost violently with her touch.

"I love you, Custis Long," she said in a barely audible whisper.

And then she pulled him down onto her.

There was a moment of resistance, and then her hymen parted and he was able to slide inside the sweet, warm depths of her.

She'd been tight. So tight. And hot. Burning hot.

And sweet.

Oh God, she'd been sweet.

So dear and gentle and giving.

She clung to him that evening, her arms wrapped tight around him while Custis rooted and grunted atop her, trying his best to be slow and gentle with her, but driven half into frenzy by the feel of her body surrounding and engulfing him, and quickly, much too quickly, the pressure rose and the blood boiled and the hot juices spurted out of him in wave after teeth-cracking, toe-curling wave, until she surely was full to overflowing with all he put into her. And still Janet held onto him and kissed him and lovingly, dearly gave of herself to him.

And the second time, bless her, had been even better than the first, and then . . .

Longarm groaned aloud as the memories washed through him like waves crashing onto a stormy seashore.

He stood on a sidewalk in the business district of Fairplay, Colorado, a man grown and a man alone, and wondered if he'd been a complete damned fool all those long years back when he'd decided, coldly and deliberately, that he would not ride back again to the place he'd once called home.

Chapter 6

"Mind that you're there at the time an' date it says on the paper, Mr. Warnett, or the judge'll issue a bench warrant an' I'll have to come up an' fetch you down in manacles. Wouldn't neither one of us want that, I think."

The businessman shrugged, taking no offense at the warning, and said, "I will be there, Deputy. They only want me to testify to what I saw, and as long as I tell the truth I don't have to worry about that, do I?"

"No, sir, I reckon that's all anyone will want of you." Longarm smiled and touched the brim of his hat as he turned to leave Warnett's shop. "Good day, sir."

"And to you, Deputy." Warnett went back to a set of ledgers laid out on the counter and Longarm stepped outside.

He paused on the sidewalk in the bright but oddly cool high country sunshine and lit a cheroot, then dragged the bulbous Ingersoll from his vest pocket and checked the time of day. Just past noon. He still had time to fetch his gear from the hotel and make it over to the depot for the afternoon run to Leadville by way of Alma and Mosquito Pass.

Mr. Warnett's had been the last of his subpoenas to be served in Park County, so now he was free to cross over to the Arkansas River valley and finish up this assignment.

After that, well, a man never knew. One thing sure. Billy Vail seldom allowed any of his deputies to become bored. There was always something that needed to be done.

Longarm drew deep of the clean flavor of the smoke, and ambled off in the direction of the hotel.

He was nearing the bank building—and thinking once again about Janet Brennan and all that might have been—when he damn near got run over by someone racing past.

The man stumbled, righted himself, and glared back over his shoulder at Longarm.

"In a mighty big hurry ain't you, Ed?" Longarm grumbled aloud. "You like to knocked me down."

"I'll do worse than that if you think you can horn in this time, damn you, Long. You have no jurisdiction here. Not this time. So get the hell out of my town." Kramer glowered at him, then spun around and once more broke into a run to make it the last few paces to the bank building.

Longarm thought about going on by. After all, if he dallied overlong, he would miss his connection to Leadville and have to wait for the night coach—he hated crossing Mosquito Pass at night—or all the way until morning.

Still, the town marshal's behavior did have Longarm's curiosity at full gallop.

Something was up, and Longarm wondered what it might be.

And in truth, the fact that whatever it was was taking place in Harry Faire's bank added an extra dab of interest to the question since it might well effect Janet as well as Harry and their depositors.

On an impulse, then, Longarm turned and followed Town Marshal Ed Kramer into the tall and dignified red-brick bank building.

•   •   •

Longarm's stomach did a somersault and his heart felt like it skipped a couple beats when he saw a man bending over a supine form on the floor of the bank lobby.

The man with the black bag was quite obviously a doctor. And the person he was working on so intently was a woman.

Longarm recognized the dress the woman was wearing. He'd sat across a table having coffee with the owner of that dress not two hours past.

Something was very seriously wrong with Janet Brennan Faire.

Longarm moved closer to get a better look. The doctor, for reasons of delicacy that Longarm found to be antiquated and indeed quite stupid, was trying to treat Janet without exposing the flesh of her belly to view. Instead the man was reaching into the gap created by opening a single button and was probing about with his hands. Hands which were, Longarm soon saw, smeared a bright and sticky scarlet with blood.

Janet had been injured somehow. And in such a way as to draw blood.

Marshal Ed Kramer was off to one side talking with a slightly built man with salt-and-pepper gray in his beard. It took Longarm a minute to realize that this distinguished-looking fellow was Hairy Harry the Fairy of so very long ago.

Christ, Longarm thought, what a stupid nickname that one had been.

Hurtful as hell to its bearer, probably, although no one would have given consideration to that back when they were kids.

A stupid nickname stupidly—and in a manner of speaking innocently—arrived at.

It had been the summer they were all—he tried to remember—thirteen? Along about then. Had to be.

They, a pack of boys who ran loosely together, had taken bag lunches and fishing poles and gone on a lark. The fishing hadn't been worth a damn, so they all stripped off and went swimming instead.

Poor Harry, never particularly big or robust, hadn't yet grown any pubic hair. The other boys had. And so Harry was given the name Hairy in one of those left-handed jibes in which the obvious is denied. That wouldn't have been so bad really, Hairy Harry. Except some snide and snippish wit—it wasn't Longarm, but he thought he remembered who it likely was—added the Fairy part.

Hell, it was just intended as a play on words. Probably. But it was cruel. Undeniably cruel.

After all, there wasn't anything wrong with Harry or really all that much different. Shit, he simply was slower than the rest of the bunch to grow hair on his balls. There was no big deal about that.

Yet because of a bit of stupid wordplay, Harold Faire was tagged with a nickname so derogatory that its origin was quickly forgotten and its bearer became a virtual outcast from the rest of the group.

Stupid, Longarm realized now that he was able to look back on it with the accumulated wisdom—well, a little bit of it anyhow—and the increased objectivity of passing years.

Stupid indeed, he thought now.

Anyway, now that he got a good look, he could see that the man in the handsomely tailored gray suit and perfectly tied necktie was indeed Harry Faire.

Harry was crying. Talking in halting fits and starts. Wringing his hands and dabbing at his eyes and babbling on while Ed Kramer listened.

And on the floor, dammit, a doctor was taking his fucking time about seeing to Janet's wounds.

Longarm had no idea what had taken place here. But he was mighty interested in finding out.

He sidled closer, coming up behind Kramer so the local lawman would be unlikely to notice Longarm's intrusion.

That was because unfortunately Marshal Ed Kramer had been entirely within his rights when he'd said Deputy Marshal Custis Long had no jurisdiction here.

Not until or unless some competent local authority invited participation by the federal officer.

Longarm resolved to stay just as meek and agreeable as a kitten if that was what it took, just so he could find out what happened to Janet. And if there was anything he could do to help her now.

Chapter 7

"There was no . . . they didn't have to . . . oh, Jesus God, why did they do that?" Faire was shaking and blubbering and looked to be on the verge of falling completely to pieces.

Ed Kramer touched him on the shoulder, not shaking him but comforting him, and said, "It's all right, Harry. Do me a favor now. Start over. Right from the beginning. Take your time and tell me everything that happened, every little thing that you can remember."

The town marshal's instruction was good on two levels, Longarm recognized. Retelling a story already told could sometimes add detail to what was said. But more important right now, the retelling of something familiar could help bring calm to the distraught. Longarm wouldn't have given Kramer credit for knowing the technique if he hadn't heard it himself. Not that that was reason enough to grant the son of a bitch any respect. But still . . .

"I was . . . they didn't have to . . . "

"It's all right now, Harry. Take a deep breath. That's right. Now tell me. Everything. Right from the start," Kramer prompted in a low, gentle tone, again reaching out to clasp Faire's shoulder in a gesture of calm and comfort.

Harry Faire—he had changed over the years, matured immeasurably—took a long, deep breath and visibly struggled to regain control over his emotions. He continued to tremble. But perhaps a little less so.

"There were three of them," he said slowly. "They came in . . . I don't know how long it's been now. What time is it?" No one paid any attention to the question, and Faire did not bother waiting for an answer.

"They were rough-looking men. Dirty. Unshaven. Like they'd been on the road for a long time. You know? Dressed like cowboys, not mining men. High heels on their boots. Big hats instead of caps. Like that. You know?" Again he did not actually expect an answer.

"Three of them. Did I say that already? One had long hair. Very dirty. Brown, I think. They all had mustaches. One of them had a dark smear beside his nose. A scar, I suppose. Very hard-looking men. Ugly. And they all had guns. I don't like guns. Never have. They all carried pistols. Big ones.

"They came in . . . let me see. Otis Valentine was at the counter. He was here to draw out the week's payroll for the Wayeth Group mines. Otis does that about this same time every week. He's always the first to pick up his payroll cash. Likes to give his clerks time to sort everything out and make up little envelopes to hand out. Most like to count the payroll out as it's ticked off the roll, but Otis doesn't like his workers to know what anyone else earns. So he takes his cash out early and has these envelopes made up ready to be handed out as the man announces himself. You know?"

Kramer didn't say anything. And behind him, Longarm kept his mouth carefully shut too.

"I think . . . I think maybe these men knew who Otis was and what he was here for. I think they may have timed their robbery so all the payroll money for all the businesses we serve would still be in the vault. I mean, they came in and one of them, the shortest of them, walked over behind Otis and smiled at him like he knew Otis and told Otis that his business would have to wait, that he couldn't take out any money this week due to insufficient funds. He . . . he sort of laughed when he said that.

"Elaine . . . she was behind the counter, of course, waiting on Otis . . . Elaine got mad when she heard the man say that. I suppose she thought the fellow was saying something insulting about our bank, like we wouldn't have enough funds on deposit to cover the needs of business, something like that. But of course the man knew exactly what he meant. He was saying there wouldn't be any money available because he and the other two were going to take it all with them. They . . ." Faire's face twisted as he remembered, and Kramer gave him just a moment to calm down again and then asked him to go on.

"Yes. Sorry." Harry took another long, slow breath and shivered a little, then sighed and dabbed at his eyes before continuing.

"The men, all three of them, pulled out their pistols and cocked them and ordered Otis to get down on the floor face-down and not to look up. The man was pointing the barrel of his pistol right into Otis's face when he said that. Otis got down on the floor just like he said, and as far as I know didn't look up again afterward. I can't blame him. I . . . I was over there in my office. I could see what was going on through the glass. But I couldn't . . . I don't own a gun, you see. And who would have thought . . ."

"You're doing just fine, Harry," Ed Kramer encouraged.

"Yes, well, anyway . . . the man at the counter pointed his gun at Elaine and told her to give him all the money and she did. I always told her that the money isn't as important as she is, so if something like this should ever happen she should just do whatever she was told and everything would be all right. Oh, God, I told her that. I told her everything would be all right." Faire began to sob again.

"Everything will be all right, Harry. You'll see." It

might well have been a lie—it was much too early to know about that—but if so the lie seemed to work. At least a little. Harry Faire took another deep breath and managed to calm himself again.

"While that first man was taking the money Elaine had in the drawer, the other two came around behind the counter and started gathering everything in the vault. They walked inside and swept things off the shelves and into their bags."

"Bags? What bags?" Kramer asked. Longarm would have asked the same question.

"They . . . they all had bags with them. Didn't I mention that? No? Well, they did. They each were carrying a burlap sack. Feed sacks, I think. They put the money in those. And then one of them, one behind the counter, pointed at Elaine and said something to the one who was with him . . . I couldn't hear what he said, didn't have to, of course . . . and both of them laughed and then the one who'd spoken first looked at the leader, who was still outside the counter, and said, 'That teller is kinda pretty. Let's take her along for company, hey?' and the leader frowned and said no, but the other two acted like they didn't want to be told what to do even if that other man was in charge, and the one who first got the idea went over and took Elaine by the wrist and started pulling her toward the gate there, toward the pass-through into the lobby. And then . . . oh, God."

"You're doing fine, Harry, just fine."

"Then Janet . . . she had come in just a few minutes earlier, later than she usually got to work . . . she'd come in just a few minutes before and was in the back getting her sleeve protectors on and like that . . . she came out in time to see this filthy, ugly creature hauling Elaine away, and Janet shouted something at him and . . . and sort of lunged at the fellow . . . and the man . . . the man . . . oh, God, Ed . . . the man shot her. He didn't have to do that. He shouldn't have . . . he turned and sort of, I don't know, he sort of flinched. And his gun was pointing at Janet. And the gun went off and she made a sound like . . . like she

36

was coughing, sort of. And she grabbed hold of her stomach and sat down. Right there on the floor. Her legs gave out from under her and she just dropped down right there on the floor, right there where she is right now. And then . . . it all sort of runs together after that. I . . . I remember kneeling beside Janet and crying, but I don't remember how I got from my office to there at her side. And I sort of remember the men running out. They took the bags of money, of course, and they . . ." Harry frowned, concentrating in thought. "I think they picked Elaine up, one of them did, and carried her out too. I don't think she ran with them, I think the one who liked her picked her up bodily and put her over his shoulder and carried her out that way. And I . . . I don't remember much else after that. Somebody . . . Otis, I suppose . . . ran out to find the doctor. And then you came in. And then . . . I just don't know, Ed. I just don't know what happened after that." Faire broke down and began crying again.

Looking down at Janet, so pale and anguished as she lay on the red tile flooring of the bank lobby, Longarm felt close to it himself.

Damn them. Damn the sons of bitches who'd done this anyway, Longarm thought.

Chapter 8

"Custis? Custis?" Janet's voice was surprisingly strong. Both Harry Faire's and Ed Kramer's heads snapped about in response. Kramer looked interested, but her husband's expression was one of hurt and of deep sadness.

"Do you think she's trying to tell us who shot her?" the town marshal asked in a hoarse whisper too low for Janet to hear.

Faire shook his head. "She's delirious," he said. "That's the name of a neighbor she hasn't seen since we were kids."

"Custis," Janet repeated. "Help me."

Longarm left his position behind Kramer and went to her, kneeling at her side.

"Who the hell . . ." Harry blurted out.

"Longarm, get outa here," Kramer barked. "I already told you that you aren't welcome."

Faire, however, came closer, bending down to peer into Longarm's face. "My God," he said after a moment's intense scrutiny. "It *is* you. You've filled out. You used to be such a skinny, gawky kid. But it really is you. I can see that now. How did you . . . ?"

Longarm took Janet's hand in his and squeezed it gently. Then, to her husband, he said, "I ran into Janet on the street this morning by accident. We had coffee at the hotel. Caught up on old times. I . . . I wish to God, Harry, that we'd sat there and talked another hour or so."

"But you . . ."

"She told me how well you're doing, how proud she is o' you an' your daughter. Now this." Longarm shook his head and stared down at Janet. He was surprised to see that she was looking back at him quite calmly and rationally despite her wound.

"Custis, you have to help me. Harry, you have to let him. Custis, tell Harry what you've been doing these past few years."

"I'm a lawman, Harry. Federal officer."

"He hunts down criminals, Harry," Janet said. "He can help you get Elaine back from those men."

"No he can't, Miz Faire," Kramer put in. "I'm the law here, not him."

Janet ignored the local lawman and looked straight into Longarm's eyes. "I know you can do it, Custis. It . . . I am dying. No, don't bother denying it. I feel all churned up inside. No, don't try to stop me, either one of you. I know, you want me to be quiet and rest and get better and all that silly drivel that we tell people who are dying. Except I will not get better. Don't you think I have seen stomach wounds before now? Of course I have. No one recovers from a gunshot like this, and by tonight I will be in so much pain that I may not be able to talk to you sensibly. I want both of you to listen to me now while the shock of the injury is keeping the pain away. Both of you listen to what I have to say while I can still say it.

"Harry, next to you Elaine is the most precious thing to me in all the world. I love her more than I could begin to tell you. And I will *not* lie here and allow those men to get away with taking her from me. I simply will not do that.

Besides, Harry, with me dead you will need Elaine to take care of you. She will, you know. She loves you almost as much as you love her. And Harry dear, I know how very much you truly do love Elaine. Well, you will need her later as much as she needs you now. You and Custis. I want . . . I know this will be hard for you, dear, but I want you to let Custis help you get Elaine back.

"And Custis, I want you to help Harry. And me. I . . . I don't have much time, Custis, but I will try to hang on until Elaine is safe. I want to know that she is all right before I die."

"Sweetheart, you aren't going to . . ."

"Hush, dear, of course I am going to die. Probably quite badly at that. They will want to give me laudanum or whatever to stop some of the pain. In fact, I almost hope they will. But . . . Harry dear, even if I beg for release, don't let them let me die. Not until Elaine is home. Then let me see her so I can slip away happy and at peace. Will you do that for me, please, dear?"

Faire was on the floor at Janet's other side, holding her other hand. He was weeping openly now. Not that Longarm blamed him. Longarm kinda felt like it his own self.

Because of course Janet was right. If her wound was indeed a belly wound . . .

Not that the prissy asshole of a doctor had really found that out yet, Longarm thought. Maybe the injury wasn't so bad after all. Maybe . . . maybe they should find out and never mind the doctor's stupid fumbling around underneath layers of cloth when what was really needed was a good look-see.

Longarm brought out his penknife and used its sharp blade to slice through Janet's dress and undergarments, exposing the pale, tender flesh of her belly.

There—dammit—was a dime-sized purple depression a few inches below her navel.

The ugly little blemish appeared innocent enough. There was no longer any blood to speak of.

But around it the skin was discolored and swollen. And inside there would be damage beyond belief.

40

Longarm had seen wounds like this before. They were the most terrible that anyone could suffer. They destroyed a person's insides and resulted in a death so pain-wracked and horrid that the strongest of strong men were reduced to begging for the mercy of death. And the agony could drag on for days.

Janet knew that. She knew it and she was willing to suffer through it for however long it would take for her daughter to be returned to safety.

If, that is, it would prove possible for Elaine to be found and rescued alive.

The robbers could well choose to rape the girl and kill her immediately rather than risk being found with her in their possession.

After all, ordinary citizens will often shrug when they think about someone who has robbed a rich and faceless institution—a bank, say, or a railroad.

But raging mobs, hellbent on retribution, are apt to form when an innocent girl is raped.

The kidnappers would surely know that.

It would be in their own best interests for the men to take their pleasure with Elaine quickly and kill her soon.

Probably, Longarm thought, there was scant expectation that Elaine would live to see another sunrise.

Unless perhaps . . . "Harry."

"Yes, Custis?"

"We have to talk, you and me."

"About . . . ?"

"In private, Harry. You and me need t' have some words in private."

"Damn you, Longarm," Ed Kramer injected.

"I know, dammit, you got jurisdiction here an' I don't."

"That's right and don't you forget it. I—"

"Ed, let me ask you something. What's more important right now? Jurisdiction or that girl's life?"

"Why, there can't be any question about that. Naturally."

"Naturally," Longarm agreed. "So shut your mouth an' let me have a talk with Harry for a few minutes."

41

"Custis," Janet said.

"I know, Janet. I know." Longarm squeezed her hand, then stood and motioned for Harry to join him.

There was only one small office inside the bank that offered any degree of privacy. That was Harry's office. Longarm headed for it, confident Harry would follow.

Chapter 9

"You bastard!" Harry Faire shouted as he stormed out of the office with Longarm trailing lamely along behind. "You don't care anything about Elaine, Custis. You only care about yourself. My God, man, you haven't changed in all these years. You were arrogant and selfish and cruel when we were kids, and you still are, damn you. Now just . . . get out. Get out of here. Out of my bank, out of my town, out of my life."

At least Janet did not have to hear any of that outburst, Longarm thought. The doctor had had her carried off, presumably for treatment, while Longarm and Harry were closeted in the bank president's private office.

At least there was that to be grateful for.

Ed Kramer, on the other hand, was obviously getting quite a kick out of Faire's anger toward Longarm.

"What was that you were saying about jurisdiction, Ed?" Harry demanded loudly.

Kramer was more than happy to repeat the short lesson for Harry's benefit.

"Do you know what he was doing in there, Ed? Do you?" Harry bellowed practically at the top of his lungs. "He was running you down. Huh! Trying to build himself up is more like it. He wants the glory for himself if there is any. And wants to place blame for the robbery on you. Can you believe it? It is . . . disgusting, that's what it is. Disgusting and reprehensible. And this is the man my wife wants to take charge of the search for our daughter? I think not."

"Let me tell you what I—"

"Yes, yes, of course, Ed, whatever you think. But let me tell *you* a few things first. Elaine is my only child, and I *will* have her back. Do you understand me? I want to post a reward for her safe return. Twenty thousand in gold coin, Ed. Where is Morris? Have you seen Anthony Morris?" Longarm had no idea who this Morris fellow was, but Harry certainly seemed anxious of a sudden to see him.

"I told my boys to keep everybody outside, Mr. Faire," Kramer said.

"If Morris is out there, Ed, tell them to let him in immediately."

"I don't think . . ." Longarm ventured, but Harry was not listening. He gave Longarm a cold look and turned his back on the tall deputy.

Kramer went to the bank door and spoke to an officer standing guard there. A moment later he returned, a portly, balding man following close on his heels.

"There you are, Anthony. Good man. I knew you wouldn't be far, not when there is important news happening. When is your next edition due out, eh? Friday morning, right? I can't wait that long for what I have to say. Can you put out a special edition, Anthony? I'll pay for it, of course. News of the robbery here and, most important, news about the reward I'm posting for the safe return of my daughter. Twenty thousand, Anthony. In gold. All coin, all of it untraceable. What d'you say to that, eh? Twenty thousand. I want everyone in the county to know before

44

nightfall. Can you do that, Anthony? Can you?''

Longarm sighed. Harry Faire had the bit between his teeth and was acting like a mad runaway.

While Harry continued to rant and wave his arms wildly about, Longarm approached Ed Kramer. "Looks like you win this time, Ed. Damn you.''

Kramer sneered, showing yellowed teeth and emitting breath so bad it would have stopped a charging bear. "Damn right I do, Long. Now get out of here, will you? I have work to do.''

Reluctantly, but with little choice in the matter, Longarm turned away and left the bank.

There didn't seem much he could do there. Hell, there was nothing he could do there. But perhaps he could find out where they'd taken Janet. See if he couldn't find a flower garden to raid. Something.

Behind him Harry was still loudly expounding for the benefit of the local press. Hammering over and over at the point that he was willing to pay serious money for the safe return of his beloved daughter.

If she wasn't already dead, that is. If the poor girl wasn't already raped and murdered at the whim of some rotten little asshole of a bank robber.

Longarm stepped outside and paused on the sidewalk for a cheroot. Then he set off in search of a flower patch. Not that he actually intended to steal the posies if he found any. No, he would approach the owner and ask if he could buy some. If he could find any, that is. And if he could find out where they'd taken Harry Faire's dying wife, Custis Long's one-time love. God, it was awful the way things worked out sometimes.

Chapter 10

Fairplay's finest—and only—livery offered damned small prospect to Longarm's critical eye. About all he could see in and around it were mules, burros, and a handful of thick-bodied draft horses. If the place had any saddle stock to rent, they were keeping the light horses mighty well hidden.

There did not even seem to be any light vehicles available. No buggies, surreys, springboards, or small coaches. The lightest wagon Longarm could see in the yard behind the big barn was an open ore hauler.

This was, of course, mining country where saddle horses would be nothing but an expensive liability. But still, he found it annoying. Longarm needed mobility if he intended to give Janet peace of mind—which he did, and questions of jurisdiction be damned—and that meant what he needed was an animal to ride, not one to drag along behind. Otherwise the first twisty game trail he came to would be impossible to negotiate.

Longarm stood outside, knowing better than to enter another man's barn while he had a lighted cheroot in his jaw, and called out, "Halloo the livery. Anybody home in here? Hello?"

There was no immediate response, so Longarm tried again, louder. This time, after a delay of almost a full minute, he heard noises coming from the back of the cavernous structure, and soon thereafter a bare head liberally decorated with bits of hay stems lifted into view above the wall of one of the many stalls.

"Sorry if I woke you up," Longarm apologized, although he was in fact not in the least bit sorry. Hell, it was the middle of the afternoon and no honest man should be sleeping now anyway.

"You want something, mister?" the hostler asked, tucking his shirttail into his trousers and looping his galluses over his shoulder as he emerged into the alleyway.

"I need t' rent a riding horse," Longarm told him.

"Mister, you came to the wrong place for that. All I generally have on hand is draft stock."

"You don't have a light drafter trained t' the saddle too?"

"Ayuh. Two of them. A nice, matched pair of chestnuts. They'll take a saddle and snaffle bit."

"Then I'd like t' hire one of them," Longarm said.

"Sorry," the liveryman told him.

"Pardon?"

"They're both rented out right now."

"How long will they . . . ?"

"I dunno. Gus Blane and Wiley Ferguson came in a while ago and took them so they could go along with the posse that's out hunting for the Faire girl. You heard about that, I s'pose."

"I did," Longarm admitted.

"Most of the men in town, them as could find something to ride, that is, are in the posse Marshal Kramer and our banker Mr. Faire put together," the liveryman said.

It was not exactly news. Longarm had stood silently by and watched the hastily assembled posse ride out a good half hour earlier.

Kramer had declared rather loudly, no doubt wanting to boost his own popularity in the community with a show of great resolve, that they would not return until they had Elaine with them or the kidnappers in irons . . . or draped cold and dead over their own saddles. It had been a stirring speech, Longarm thought, albeit a mite long on bullshit.

Longarm would have been considerably more impressed if any one of them had had the least idea which way they should take their cloud of dust when they thundered off in the general direction of Hoosier Pass.

As far as Longarm knew, though, no one had yet come forward to report to Kramer on the direction the bank robbers took when they left Fairplay. And without that basic information to go on, Longarm doubted the posse would accomplish much beyond giving the townsmen an excuse to yelp and thump their own chests some. He figured they would make brave noises about what they would do to those damned old kidnappers when they caught up to them, but beyond that, it was all apt to be just so much dust and blunder.

At least that was often the pattern with these local posses. Unless the lawman leading them knew what he was doing, they didn't generally accomplish much more than to vent their own spleens and make everybody feel better about the loss of whatever it was that had been taken from them.

In this case, of course, he hoped for something better. But he couldn't actually claim to expect it.

"Friend, d' you know where else a person might go t' hire a saddle animal?"

The liveryman looked him over for a moment, then cackled and admitted, "Ayuh, I do."

"Yes? Well?"

"Denver, mister. Lotsa horses for rent down to Denver, they tell me."

Longarm scowled and dragged out his wallet, flipping it open so the hostler could admire the badge pinned inside. "This is official United States government business," Longarm warned him. "Failure to cooperate carries a fine of up to five hundred dollars. Up to six months in jail too, but in truth I got t' tell you that a judge wouldn't likely go that far with you. He'd prob'ly settle for the fine alone."

"I was just funnin' you," the liveryman said. "Sorry."

"Friend, I just ain't much in the mood for funning right at this moment."

"I really don't have a saddle horse to rent you. Not a proper one, that is."

"You got anything at all that won't sulk up and freeze with a saddle on it?"

"I do, but . . ."

"But?"

"Yeah, well, this old gelding used to be a stallion. Its owner used to saddle and ride it from farm to farm when he was going off to service mares. It would take a saddle still, I think, but . . ."

"But?"

With a shrug the liveryman turned and walked away down the barn aisle. He was back a few minutes later leading just about the biggest sonuvabitch of an equine creature that Longarm ever laid eyes on.

The horse stood close to eighteen hands tall, and was so wide it likely couldn't fit between the shafts of a cart or small rig. No wonder the owner wouldn't have used a stud cart when he was traveling with this old boy; the damn thing would have been too broad to fit. Unless he was yoked, that is. He was built heavier than most oxen.

Longarm looked at the thing and groaned. With a back that broad, a man would find himself doing a split in order to ride it. Either that or settle for riding sidesaddle.

"It's a shire," the hostler said. Unnecessarily. The gleaming coal-black hide, white face, and shaggy white feathers on its lower legs proclaimed its bloodline clear enough.

The horse was no youngster either. Its muzzle was grizzled dirty white with age, and its teeth were yellowed and worn.

Still and all . . .

"His name is George," the liveryman said. "He won't take you no place in a hurry. But old George, he's hell for durable. You might get him to raise a sweat if you asked him to pull a railroad car for ten or twelve hours straight. But there's nothing short of that will slow him down. Nor, for that matter, speed him up. Load him up as heavy as you like, climb on top of the pile, and point him in the direction you want him to go, and George will take you there. Eventually.''

The hostler came closer, leading George with him, and jabbed Longarm sharply in the breastbone with a pointing finger. "One more thing," he said. "This is a good old horse, solid and honest and true. If you abuse him, mister, federal marshal or not, I promise I'll whip your ass when you get back.''

The liveryman was half a head shorter than Longarm and a good twenty years older. That didn't make any difference. He meant exactly what he said, and Longarm respected the intention of the warning even if he was not especially alarmed by it.

"I'll take good care o' the old fella for you, friend.''

The hostler grunted softly and turned to scratch George in the sensitive hollow beneath his jaw, then affectionately rubbed the old horse's poll.

"Wait here, mister. I'll suit him up for you.''

Longarm nodded. It occurred to him that they hadn't yet gotten around to talking about price.

Not that it really mattered. He would pay whatever the liveryman asked. Out of his own pocket if it came to that.

It was that important to him.

Chapter 11

A couple years back—three? something like that—Longarm made the acquaintance of a proper British gentleman.
The fellow was engaged in a round-the-world journey, and
while on the plains of the American West was busy shooting every sort of wildlife he could take under his sights.
Buffalo, elk, panthers, even specimens as insignificant as
prairie dogs and burrowing owls, just about anything that
walked, crawled, or flew. The idea was to collect and mount
all the critters and haul them back for scientific study.

Longarm suspected the main reason was that the Englishman just liked to hunt game, but the fellow was a
friendly sort and stocked his camp with all the comestibles,
cigars, and whiskey anyone could ask. Longarm had en-
joyed visiting with him.

What brought that man back to mind now was something
he'd said about hunting tigers in India. It was done from
the backs of elephants, he'd sworn.

Apparently the shooter and the guide rode in these little

houses—called a howdy or something close to it, if Long-arm remembered correctly—that they strapped onto the elephant's back.

There was supposed to be room in there for the hunter and guide and a gun loader, and then outside the little house, sitting kind of on the elephant's neck, the elephant driver, whatever he was called, rode.

The Englishman said those howdy things were downright comfortable, shady and with benches and pillows and such built right in.

Longarm hadn't gone two miles aboard old George the Shire before he got to thinking that what he needed for this trip was one of those howdy things to strap onto the son-uvabitch's back.

As it was he was seated—perched was more like it—atop a moving surface about the width of an ordinary bed. Definitely wider than a bunkhouse cot.

The horse was so wide there was no way a man could sit astride it in a normal manner. If a person managed to get one foot down to stirrup level, the other leg pretty much had to be pulled up on top of George's back, either stretched out alongside the horse's neck or else curled up underneath the rider like a young girl would sit on the end of a sofa. Try and spread a fellow's legs wide enough apart to take a normal seat, and he was sure to mash his balls to jelly any time George lumbered into a trot. Which, in truth, seemed to be a somewhat seldom happenstance anyhow, and therefore not too much of a threat.

Longarm had never seen a saddle wide enough to fit on a boardinghouse bed, and the Fairplay livery hadn't had one either. What passed as a saddle for use on George was a canvas-backed, quilted affair with oxbow stirrups hanging from canvas straps and more canvas webbing to take the oversized cinches. Neither leather nor a rigid saddle tree had been used to put the rig together, and as saddles went this one pretty much looked like hell.

On the other hand, it worked. With it Longarm could, with a mite of stretching and straining, get a boot into a stirrup and climb onto the big shire. Without benefit of the stirrups he expected he would've had to carry a stepladder along with him. But then, hell, there was room enough across George's butt to lash a stepladder, some suitcases, and whatever other luggage a man might want to tote.

Anyway, it was possible to stay atop the pokey old thing. And riding something, riding anything, beat walking. Every time. Longarm decided he should forget about niggling details and pay attention to business.

There were two reasons Longarm chose to head south once he got the big horse to moving.

One was that Ed Kramer and his posse had taken off toward the north, toward Alma, Hoosier Pass, Breckenridge, and points beyond. Longarm figured the exact opposite of that should be his to look into.

The second reason, however, was even stronger. Instead of leaping into the saddle—such as it was—and larruping away in a lather, Longarm idled about on the streets a bit before he made up his mind what to do.

And as luck would have it, the same sort of luck that seemed to follow anyone who paid attention to business, he'd had a brief chat with a boy of twelve or so who'd seen the kidnappers ride out.

They'd gone south. The boy was sure of it. There were four of them, the three who went inside the bank and an outside man likely posted to hold the horses and stand guard, and they'd had Elaine Faire with them, draped across the pommel of the smallest man's saddle.

The boy had been so excited that he hadn't even blushed when he told Longarm that he remembered seeing the girl in particular because her dress blew halfway up her limbs when the men quirted their horses, and he could see not only her ankles but the shape of her calf near as high as her knee as well. That was undoubtedly the most flesh the horny kid had ever seen in his life. Longarm hoped the sight didn't corrupt him overmuch.

Anyway, with that to go on, Longarm sawed and yanked at George's reins—unnaturally short driving lines was more like it—until he had the horse aimed in the direction he wanted, then bounced and whacked and chirped to the creature until it was moving, eventually getting the animal up to the dizzying speed of a slow trot.

He hoped to hell this search didn't come down to any kind of a chase. Catching up with anybody, or running away from someone, just wasn't apt to be in the cards here.

Chapter 12

"H'lo, gents," Longarm greeted, reining George to a grateful halt. The wagon drivers likewise stopped.

There were two of them. Wagons, that is. With four men sprawled across the seats. Both were light farm-type rigs, each drawn by a mismatched pair of light cobs that showed about as much wild barb as draft stock in their blood.

They were coming north on the road that led through Hartsel and eventually down through Trout Creek Pass to Buena Vista and the Arkansas River, or east past Pikes Peak to Manitou, Colorado City, and such. Either of those directions would find a railroad track, and Longarm guessed that these young men had given up on mining. The placer deposits in this part of the country had played out long ago, and nowadays it was all rich-man mining going on, heavy on equipment and capitalization and short on individual initiative. The men might well have gone back to the farming they'd learned as boys. Damned hard work at this altitude, farming, although Longarm understood a man could grow cold-resistant crops like potatoes, cabbages, and celery here in South Park, or over east a way in the even less accessible High Park.

Anyway, whoever they were and whatever they'd delivered, the men were finished with their tasks now. The wagons were both clattering empty, save for tarpaulins bunched all stiff and muddy at the front of otherwise empty wagon boxes.

"You lost, mister?" one of the farmers asked. "Need some help?"

"I'm not lost, but I sure could use some help," Longarm admitted, rummaging through his pockets to come up with a cheroot and matches. Politeness required that he offer cheroots to the fellows on the wagons too, but only one of them accepted. "Have you heard about the trouble in Fairplay this morning?" Longarm asked.

"No, sir."

Longarm told them about the robbery and kidnapping, which led to some dropped jaws and grumbling. "Nothing like that ever happens around here, mister," one of them said.

"Well, it did this time."

"You part of a posse or something?" a man on the second wagon asked.

"No, but there's a posse out chasing after them, o' course. Me, I just thought since I seen you, I'd ask if you noticed anything that might be helpful to Marshal Kramer," Longarm told them.

"We haven't seen nothing like that. I mean, no girl being carried off or anything by fellas on horseback. Come to that, mister, you don't see so awful many men a-horseback in this part of the country. Wagons"—he pointed in the general direction of his feet to indicate the wagon he happened to be riding in—"are what you mostly see up here." The man also gave George a pointed look, but was polite enough to not come right out and say anything about the big shire and its makeshift saddle.

"Thanks anyway," Longarm said, drawing on his cheroot.

"What about . . . you know," one of the men said.

The other three shrugged and showed no particular interest, although it was obvious they all understood the comment.

"What's that?" Longarm asked.

"Probably nothing," said the fellow who'd brought the subject up for discussion.

"If it's nothing, then no harm will be done. But if it turns out to be something . . ." Longarm let the implications hang in the air unspoken.

"Yeah, well, this was maybe three quarters of a mile back," the farmer said. He twisted around on the seat and pointed. "You see that hill back there?"

"Ayuh."

"Just the other side of it, see, there's like a marsh at the foot and then a stand of quakies growing on up the slope. The face you can see is bare except for rock and grass, but around the other side there's the quakies, see."

"Uh-huh."

"Well we was too far away to get a good look. And whatever was going on, we only seen a bit of it anyhow. But what it looked like to me was two men on foot chasing after a boy."

"You're sure it was a boy?" Longarm asked.

"I thought it was a boy at the time, but come to think of it, I guess I thought that because he—or whoever—was so much smaller than the men that was running after him. Her. Whatever."

"Did anyone else see these folks?" Longarm asked.

"I did."

"So did I."

"And what was your impression?"

"I thought it was a boy too."

"Not me. I thought at the time it was a girl they were chasing. Because of the way the kid ran. Loose-kneed, like. You know what I mean?"

"Jeez, Willy, you never said any such a damn thing when we seen them. What makes you say now you thought it was a girl?"

"Because I *did,* dammit," the one called Willy protested indignantly. "Just because I never said nothing doesn't mean I didn't think it."

"Willy, you never in your whole life had a thought in your head that didn't come straight out of your mouth afterward," one of the men teased.

"Hell, Al, you can quit talking right after you say Willy never in his whole life had a thought in his head. That says it all," another put in.

Longarm figured the bunch of friends could run on in this vein for quite some time if they felt like it. And probably they did. "Gents, I thank you for your help." He touched the brim of his Stetson and prepared to thump George into motion again.

"You gonna go look for those fellas and whoever they was chasing?" one of the farmers asked.

"I dunno if I ought to do a thing like that seeing as how I'm not actually a part of the posse," Longarm said. "But I suppose it couldn't hurt if I was to look a mite closer and see if there's anything I should go tell Marshal Kramer." He grinned. "I don't reckon that would hurt anything."

The helpful farmers repeated directions so Longarm could find the place where they'd seen two people on foot chasing a third smaller person. "They looked to be headed toward the top of that hill yonder," one of them said.

"Any of you know what's over there?" Longarm asked.

"Not me."

"No."

"I remember trailing a gutshot deer over that way a spell back," another said. "There's a creek back in there and a cabin beside an adit opening. The cabin's about fallen in, and I'd say it's been a long time since anybody lived there. I never went inside the adit, so I can't tell you anything about that."

"Thanks, fellows. You've been a big help."

"Any time." The farmers laughed and waved, and the one who'd accepted a cheroot from Longarm puffed deep on it and blew some smoke rings into the air.

"Good luck, mister."

"You too, gents."

Longarm aimed George toward the hill in question and tried, with limited success, to make the horse break into a faster gait.

Chapter 13

The aspen grove was right where the farmers said it would
be. Apart from that, however, Longarm wasn't having
much luck verifying their story. There was no sign now of
anyone running around through the woods. And contrary
to what some back-East folks seemed to believe, it was
pretty nigh impossible to track someone on foot through
the western mountains.

Longarm had no idea what the ground was like back in
Kentucky and Tennessee and those places where old Dan'l
Boone once roamed, but out here in the Rockies the soil
was mostly gravel, with now and then some red clay mixed
in, and plenty of slabs of granite scattered around for good
measure.

Barring the convenience of snow on the ground, a man
might be able to trail a deer or a horse, particularly a shod
horse. But someone afoot? No way.

Longarm had to settle for doing his best, which in this
case consisted of first searching through the quaking aspens

where the farmers said they saw people running, and then taking George up and over the crown of the hill toward the drainage on the other side where the abandoned diggings were said to be located.

Longarm wasn't sure what he expected to find there.

Oh, four horses, four bank robbers, and Elaine Faire would have been extra nice to discover waiting for him on the south side of the hill.

But he didn't actually expect that. Didn't find it either.

Instead he found the tumbledown cabin he'd been told about and the dark, empty mouth of a prospect hole or mine adit.

He dismounted and stretched a mite while his legs got reacquainted; it had been quite some time since they'd been close to one another.

He tied George to an aspen sapling that was growing smack in front of the doorway to the old cabin, and checked inside. The place, what was left of it, was empty. Well, what he could see of it was empty anyway. There was one corner that he couldn't look into because parts of the roof had collapsed and were lying in his way. Longarm figured if five people could hide back there, in a space so cramped he didn't think he could wriggle into it given a bucket of grease to make himself slippery with, then they damn well deserved to stay hidden.

He backed out, thinking either the farmers were wrong about what they'd seen or else the men who'd been chasing that kid had run right on past this place.

Still, he was here now and probably should take a peek into the mine adit before he moved on.

Besides, doing some more looking around would make it that much more relief his legs and butt got before he had to scale George's heights again.

Longarm helped himself to a cheroot, and then proceeded to poke his nose into the mouth of the adit.

And damn near was treated to a shave in the process.

He hadn't much more than shown himself at the entrance than a hatchet—not a tomahawk or a shingling ax or anything remotely normal, but a strangely shaped and very

61

shiny hatchet—came whirling out of the darkness inside the adit, passing close enough to Longarm's mustache that it would have given him a trim if he'd pursed his lips and stood still for a few seconds longer.

As it was, he was tight against the stone of the entryway and had his Colt in his hand before he had time to consciously register the situation.

A *hatchet*? Who the fuck went around throwing hatchets at people in this day and age?

In a loud voice Longarm called, "Whoever you are, you have just committed an assault on a federal law officer engaged in the commission of his duties. I am obliged to inform you that that is a federal offense punishable by up to five years imprisonment and fines of up to five thousand dollars. I suggest you come out with your hands in plain sight if you want to avoid arrest and formal charges against you."

Sounded like a right fine speech, he thought, even if it was mostly bullshit.

"And don't be throwing no more damn hatchets neither."

He heard what he thought was whispering inside the adit, then the crunch of gravel underfoot.

There was only one man walking, Longarm judged, though there had to be at least two people inside. Else why would there be any whispering going on? If that was what he'd heard.

"Slow and easy," he said aloud, and then slipped back a few paces more in case someone wanted to key off the sound of his voice to place him.

Sounded like one person. Turned out to be two. Both of them moving as one, however. Which did not make Longarm feel appreciably better about misjudging it.

Two people, he thought, or more likely one and a half. The second fellow was too small to count as a whole person.

They were Chinese, both of them, Longarm saw, with long pigtails, high-collar coats, and floppy pajama trousers. One of the men was almost as tall as Longarm. The other

62

one didn't seem to come much more than belt high on the big one.

Both had dark complexions and even darker expressions. They did not appear happy to have company here.

"Hold it right there," Longarm ordered, emphasizing his request with a wave of his Colt. "Hold your hands out from your sides and turn around nice an' slow."

The small one whispered to his much larger companion, and a few seconds later both men did as Longarm instructed.

"You," he said, "the big guy. There's a bulge under your shirt. Is that a gun you're carrying? Take it out nice an' slow with just two fingers if you please. Take it out an' lay it down easy."

The small man started to say something, but Longarm snapped, "You. Quiet."

"I beg your apology, kind sir, but my estimable friend Lee Fong does not speak your language. Unless I inform him of your desires he cannot comply."

"If he reaches for that gun, little fellow, he's dead. You want to tell him that for me, please? He's to take it out with just two fingers, like I said, else I shoot."

"We mean you no harm, sir, we merely—"

"You merely tried to slice my head off with your damn hatchet. Now get him to do what I say or you'll have t' bury him."

"Yes, sir, of course, sir." The small Chinese clasped his hands together as if in prayer and bowed low toward Longarm, then turned and said something to his friend in a torrent of hisses and clacks and clatter.

The big one, Lee Fong, scowled and acted like he didn't wanta.

Longarm tapped the ash off his cheroot and then, looking Lee Fong square in the eyes, thumbed back the hammer of his revolver. That was not strictly necessary as the Colt was a double-action model. But it had a nicely menacing sound to it, which was what Longarm wanted at the moment.

The little fellow said something more and, reluctantly, Lee Fong lifted the bottom of his jacket.

It was not a gun he was carrying there, it turned out, but another hatchet, this one quite ornate with engraving on the blade and fancy silver work on the handle.

The thing hadn't only been made for pretty, however. The narrow blade appeared sharp enough to shave with.

"Drop it," Longarm said.

The little Chinese said something. Lee Fong bent and laid the hatchet on the ground with almost reverent care, as if it was as much a badge of office as a weapon.

"That's fine," Longarm said. "Now if you boys would just—"

He never got to finish the sentence.

From somewhere inside the dark adit he heard a sudden banshee shriek, and a tiny, bat-like figure came leaping out with fangs and claws bared, throwing itself at Lee Fong as if intent on tearing the tall Chinese's throat out.

Within seconds there was a melee, with Lee Fong and the little man and the bat thing all a-tangle.

Longarm had no idea what was going on, or why, but he was pretty sure he wanted it stopped before somebody came to an abrupt end.

"Stop, dammit," he roared, and fired his Colt in the air. That was not an especially good idea as the jolt of the concussive noise rattled the unshored roof of the adit and within seconds chunks of rock, some of them big enough to crush small animals, to say nothing of bare skulls, began to rain down on the three hissing, spitting combatants.

"Jeez!" Longarm grumbled.

He shoved his revolver back into its holster and waded into the fray, grabbing hair, britches, or whatever else came to hand as he tried to pull the three apart.

Chapter 14

Longarm plucked the little fellow out of the mess and gave
him a heave, sending him ass over teakettle into the darkness toward the interior of the adit, where the Chinese disappeared from view.

He grabbed Lee Fong by the back of the britches and
yanked, snatching the big Chinese off his feet so that he
was dangling facedown from Longarm's powerful right fist,
half doubled over and looking more or less like a trout on
a trout line. This did not please the Chinese a whole helluva
lot, and the man—he was tall but skinny and so didn't seem
to weigh all that much, certainly a manageable amount—
began to screech and gabble like a cat being held off the
ground by its tail.

With his left hand Longarm grabbed the pigtail of the
last critter, which turned out to be yet another Chinese, this
one young and fresh-faced, obviously the boy the farmers
said was being chased around the mountains.

The kid tried a roundhouse sweep with an inexpert left

hand, but he was so small he couldn't land the punch, not while Longarm was holding him out at arm's length. The blow swept harmlessly past, not even close enough to tap the cloth of Longarm's coat.

"Hold still, the both of you," Longarm said, giving his two reluctant prisoners each a small shake to get their attention.

The kid subsided, but Lee Fong either failed to understand or failed to comply with what Longarm thought was a perfectly reasonable instruction. Instead the tall Chinese snarled something that didn't need translating and reached underneath his tunic.

The hatchet was gone, Longarm discovered, but somewhere in there Lee had been carrying a spring-blade knife big enough that it shouldn't have been possible to hide it. But hide it Lee Fong had, and now he was bent on using the thing. It snapped open with a rather ugly snick of steel on steel, and Lee twisted, trying his level best to slice Longarm's leg open when he did so.

Longarm understood the effort without particularly admiring it.

And he'd about used up his patience with Lee Fong by now anyway.

He gave the Chinese a shove, sending the knife-wielding arm far enough out of range that the blade swished harmlessly past.

That accomplished, Longarm let go of his hold on Lee Fong and took half a step forward with his left foot, then brought his right boot up in as vicious and purposeful a kick as Longarm knew how to manage.

There wasn't anything fair or fancy about the assault. But it damn well got the job done. Longarm's boot took Lee Fong on the point of the chin and snapped his head back hard enough that the Chinese would have to consider himself mighty lucky if he survived with his neck intact.

The tall man's lights went out like a candle flame in a hurricane, and he dropped like a poleaxed shoat.

Longarm wasn't taking any chances with Lee Fong, though. Not again. He gave the kid a warning look, then scuttled sideways until he could squat, still peering hard at the young'un so as to discourage unwanted movement, and retrieve Lee's knife. It was a lock-blade model, and a well-made one. Longarm managed to work the mechanism one-handed, closed the blade, and dropped it into his pocket.

"You. In the back there. Come out here an' show yourself. I wanta know what this is all about."

After a moment's hesitation the small Chinese man stepped out of the adit into the sunlight. The fellow said something in Chinese, and the kid in Longarm's left hand bowed first to the Chinese man and then, turning, toward Longarm.

That was more like it, Longarm thought. Now things looked as if they might settle down a little. He smiled and kind of bobbed his head to the kid in a bow of sorts. He opened his mouth to speak.

And the damned kid jerked away from him, whirling about and throwing himself at the little Chinese with a shriek of rage.

"Dammit," Longarm squawked. He hustled forward to start the process of peacemaking all over again.

Chapter 15

"You!" Longarm said, aiming a finger at the smaller Chinese man; Lee Fong was still out cold on the floor at the mouth of the adit. "You speak English. I wanta know what this shit is about or you're all going to jail."

The Chinese bowed. "My apologies, esteemed sir. It was not our intention to cause you anguish."

"Never mind your intentions. Just tell me what this mess is all about."

"It is very simple, honorable one," the Chinese said. "My cousin Lee Fong wishes to regain missing property. Hence he pursues this most unworthy creature Lee Xua."

"Lee Wah? Is that Lee Wah?" Longarm demanded, shifting his attention to the small and somewhat grimy boy in his teens who was sullenly glowering, first at the smaller Chinese man, and then back at Longarm.

"Ah, most honorable sir, your pronunciation of our most difficult language is inestimably close to exactness, if I may say so. Yes, sir, this unfit being is the person known as Lee

Xua." He nodded his head in the direction of the kid, who wasn't much bigger than his name. Small as the grown man was, the boy scarcely came to the man's shoulders. The kid wouldn't stand much more than belly-button tall to Longarm, he thought. And dirty? Lee Xua looked like he'd been rolling in mud for half the day. Well, maybe he had, trying to get away from the two who'd been chasing him, Lee Fong and this other one.

"And who are you?" Longarm asked of the man.

"I introduce myself with pleasure to be Lee Chou." The little man bowed so low, Longarm figured he was in danger of overbalancing and toppling head first onto the dust-and-gravel-covered stone flooring.

"Lee Fong, Lee Chou, an' Lee Xua. You're all related somehow?"

"This is most assuredly so, exalted sir. I have the honor to be cousin to Lee Fong. Lee Xua is a"—his hands fluttered as he reached deep for an explanation in English—"a more distant relative. Far-away cousin, you would proclaim, I think so."

"So you're all kin. An' this kid Lee Xua, you say, took something that belongs t' Lee Fong, an' Lee Fong wants it back and . . . Lee Chou, your close cousin on the floor there, ol' Lee Fong, is awake an' playin' possum."

"I do not know what means this game of possum you speak of, but—"

"What I'm tellin' you, Lee Chou, is that your buddy on the floor there has woke up. I can tell it from the change in his breathing. He's pretending t' be still out cold, an' I think it might be a good idea for you t' explain to him that if he has some tricks in mind he'd best think again. If he comes up too quick, I'll put a bullet between his eyes to kinda slow him down. You hear what I'm tellin' you?"

Lee Chou bowed low, his hands clasped tight together, and said something in rapid-fire Chinese. Lee Fong remained motionless, and Lee Chou spoke again. This time the tall man frowned and sat up, shaking his head and rolling his neck from side to side for a few moments before coming to his feet. He glared at Longarm.

69

"You can tell him for me he's damn lucky t' still be alive, never mind standing there resenting a little pain. Most generally I'm not so patient with folks as come at me with hatchets an' knives an' such."

"Of course, estimable sir. I will explain this to my most worthy cousin Lee Fong." Lee Chou bowed again, then turned and launched into a lengthy spurt of gibberish, which Lee Fong returned just as hot and heavy. For a couple minutes there Longarm thought the cousins were going to have at each other, but after a bit they settled down and Lee Chou talked while Lee Fong glowered and grumped but did seem to be listening.

"Now that everybody seems t' be calmed down some," Longarm said at length, "whyn't you all stand over here where I can keep an eye on everybody at once. You too, Lee Xua. Everybody over there." His instruction was emphasized somewhat by the fact that he pointed with the muzzle of his Colt to indicate just where it was the three Chinese should gather. "That's better, thanks."

Throughout, Lee Chou was quietly translating.

"Now then. You were saying that Lee Xua has something that belongs t' Lee Fong. I want you t' tell me about this," Longarm said.

"It is not so much so that Lee Xua *has* something of the property of Lee Fong," Lee Chou explained patiently. "It is that Lee Xua *is* the property of Lee Fong."

"Par'n me?"

"When it was discovered that we, that is to say, that Lee Fong was in need of additional . . . um . . . employees in our . . . his . . . business enterprise, honored sir, Lee Fong appealed to the head of our family in the province of Kwangsi. Do you follow, noble sir?"

"Sure. You wrote home for help."

Lee Chou beamed with pleasure at the perceptiveness of his Occidental interrogator. "Exactly so, wise sir, exactly so."

"An' the home folks sent . . . ?"

Lee Chou beamed and bowed. "Lee Xua."

"As an employee?"

Lee Chou shrugged. "As a slave. No, more what you would call an indentured person. Lee Xua's father was paid a certain amount, and Lee Xua is obligated to act as the person belonging to Lee Fong for a period of ten years. More if Lee Xua's father asks more money in the future and if my most fair and humble cousin Lee Fong wishes to grant the extension at that time. Do you now see, good sir? Lee Xua sought to break the agreement without Lee Fong's permission. And after only four months of endeavor here in your country of wealth and promise. Lee Fong wishes only to recover that which is his and to require his most far cousin Lee Xua to honor the agreement made by our family elders. So you see, most excellent sir, there is no skullduggery afoot in this place, no. Only a business contract, do you not see?" Lee Chou's smile was broad and innocent. He spread his hands as if to say, see, there is nothing hidden here. It is all quite ordinary and proper.

"One thing," Longarm said. "Slavery ain't legal here. Or hadn't you heard?"

"But good sir, the contract we wish to enforce is not American slavery but Chinese business."

"Yeah, I see your point, but the fact is, as long as you're on American soil you got to follow American laws. So what it comes down to, gents, is that Lee Xua there is free t' come or go, whatever he wants. You boys can't stop him if he wants t' walk out an' that's that."

Lee Chou frowned.

"Tell him for me, please. Tell Lee Fong that he's gotta back off an' let Lee Xua alone."

"He will not like—"

"You ain't been paying attention, have you. Lee Chou, I don't give a fat rat's ass what Lee Fong likes or don't like. Fact is, I still might take a notion to put him in irons an' cart him off t' jail for trying t' open my skull up an' let the air an' the sunlight in. Now tell him what I said. And tell him t' stand well clear o' both me an' Lee Xua after he gets the word. You do that now, hear?"

Lee Chou didn't much like the instruction. That was

plain enough in his expression. But however reluctantly, he engaged in a lengthy discourse in Chinese.

Lee Fong looked so pissed off Longarm expected to see smoke rising out of the tall man's collar at any moment. Lee Xua, on the other hand, looked downright smug.

After a bit Lee Fong interrupted and said something, and after that the kid lost the smug look and commenced to cringe and tremble. Longarm didn't need a translation to work that one out—in general, if not as to the particulars of Lee Fong's threats.

"Something else you can tell him," Longarm said to Lee Chou.

"Yes, exalted sir?"

"Tell him, an' Lee Xua too, that when I ride outa here I'm taking Lee Xua with me. In protective custody, so t' speak. There won't be no sneaking around an' kidnapping anybody once my back is turned. You got it?"

Lee Chou bowed and scraped a bit, then turned and gave Lee Fong the word. Lee Fong got pissed off all over again—a fact that did not break Longarm's heart—and Lee Xua began to look rather smug once more.

"All right, dammit, get out o' here before I decide to run the both of you in on federal charges just t' make sure you won't be sneaking up behind me for the next two or three years."

Lee Chou bowed. Lee Fong glared. Lee Xua looked about ready to break into song and dance. And moved over to stay close to Longarm while doing so.

As for Longarm, he did not feel like tempting the fates any further than he already had. He gathered up the two hatchets that the Chinese had thrown his way and, kicking around through the grass until he located the hole where a well once served the tumbledown mine shack, tossed both hatchets, including Lee Fong's fancy and undoubtedly expensive one, into the void. Judging from how long it took for the hatchets to hit bottom, Longarm figured the old well shaft to be sixty feet deep or more. Deep enough to discourage the Chinese gents from diving in after their lethal possessions anyhow. As for Lee Fong's spring-blade knife,

Longarm kind of liked it. He left it in his pocket. If Lee Fong insisted on getting it back, he could go to Denver and petition the courts there for the return of his confiscated property. He had, after all, the right to do that under American law.

"G'day, gents," Longarm said with a swipe of one fingertip across the brim of his Stetson. "An' if you got the sense God gave a housefly, you won't even think about following me, you hear?"

"It is as you say, your munificence," Lee Chou returned.

"Yeah. Sure." Longarm climbed awkwardly onto George's wagon-sized back, then reached down to take Lee Xua by the wrist and drag the kid up onto George's broad butt. "Remember," he said. "Stay clear o' me. The both of you." He did not wait for an answer, just thumped George into plodding motion and headed more or less back the way he'd come.

The one half-assed lead he'd had turned out to be nothing more than a Chinese mess, and now there was not enough daylight left for him to accomplish anything brilliant. If he'd had any brilliant ideas to pursue, that is. So he figured to make a wide loop back in the direction of Fairplay and see if he could luck into some clues as to the whereabouts of the bank robbers. And Elaine Faire.

Lordy, he thought as he rode, he hoped the pain hadn't hit Janet yet.

It would soon enough. He knew that. There would be no avoiding it. But not yet. Please God, not yet.

Chapter 16

Southwest of Fairplay, on a rocky slope overlooking a meandering trout stream, Longarm found some fresh-looking scrape marks in the gravel. They could indicate which way the robbers had fled once they were out of town. The marks could just as easily signal a spot where last night some drunken prospector on his way home fell off his horse. There simply was no way to tell.

And whatever the cause, there was precious little daylight remaining now, thanks partially to the big shire's glacial gait. Longarm was not going to run anyone down aboard George, not even with only one person aboard, never mind two.

As for the Chinese kid, he hadn't said a word since Longarm got him onto the horse. And Longarm had no idea in hell just what he was going to do with a Chinese kid now that he had one in hand. Keep the kid safe from his cousins. That was as far as Longarm had worked that one out.

"It's time we head back t' town," Longarm said in a companionable tone, although he did not know if the kid spoke English or not. As far as he could recall, all the boy's screaming and carrying on had been undertaken in Chinese. "It will be dark soon, and I wanta find out how Mrs. Faire is doing. Besides, there might be word from the posse. I don't really expect anything from that direction, but hell, miracles do happen, y'know."

The kid sat on George's rump with all the stoic silence expected of an inscrutable Celestial. Not that Longarm cared. "Hang on, Lee Xua. We'll be in town quick as this old horse can get us there." He smiled and added, "Which means we might could make it by Thursday." Longarm thumped George's ribs with the sides of his boots—no point in provoking the poor old thing with spurs; it wasn't George's fault he was incapable of producing speed, and the old boy was certainly willing to give whatever he could—and aimed him back toward Fairplay.

Janet Faire had been moved from the doctor's office to her own home, where she could die in surroundings as peaceful and loving as possible. When Longarm called to see how she was, Harry was out somewhere—probably just as well, considering how Janet's husband seemed to feel toward her old boyfriend—and she was being attended by a pair of clucking hens who introduced themselves as Miss So-and-so and Mrs. This-or-that. Longarm made no effort to get the names straight. They were from Janet and Harry's church, they explained, and they, along with others from the Ladies Bible Society, would keep a twenty-four hour watch over Janet. The marshal did *not* need to concern himself, thank you.

Longarm thought he could detect some implied sniffing and snorting and lifting of noses into the air when they told him he was not needed, so apparently there'd been some talking in town about Harry's outburst in the bank earlier. Longarm was not surprised. A tad hurt, perhaps. But not surprised.

He insisted on looking in on Janet, and was allowed to

75

do so, probably on the theory that letting him have a peek would eliminate any excuse that he stay. He was allowed to the door of her room on the condition that he not try to interrogate her or bother her in any way. And both church ladies, prim and proddy in defense of their friend, stood by to see that this stranger not violate the terms of his parole.

It broke Longarm's heart to see Janet lying there, unresponsive and pale under a heap of down comforters. She looked small. And almost as young as when he'd last seen her, back before the big unpleasantness in the East. The effects of the wound seemed to have let the air out of her, so that now she seemed about half the size as when they'd talked this morning.

But then an awful lot had changed since then. Not very damned much of it for the better.

"Thank you, ladies," Longarm said, stepping back a step and touching his forehead before turning away.

God, he hoped Janet could find peace and a degree of comfort before she died. God, he hoped they could recover Elaine before then. Alive if that would prove to be possible, however unlikely it in all practicality seemed to be.

Longarm headed back toward his hotel room, where he'd left the Chinese kid for safekeeping.

The best thing to do this evening, he decided as he walked, was to buy something to eat and take it up to the room with him.

He was perfectly willing to knock heads if somebody wanted to object to the idea of a lowly Chinese eating in the same restaurant as white folks. But dammit, tonight he just didn't have the energy to put up with the hassle. Tonight, he figured, it was best to take the easy way out and carry their dinners up to his room instead.

Chapter 17

Longarm tugged the bell cord, and a few minutes later a huffing, panting bellboy arrived to ask what was needed.

"You can take these dishes down for us, please, an' bring back a pitcher o' hot water. Good and hot, mind. I don't feel like having a cold bath."

"Yes, sir," the bellboy said, peering beyond Longarm to the Chinese kid, who was perched in a stiffly uncomfortable pose on the room's only chair. "Will that, uh, will that be all for you, sir?"

"Just the water, thanks."

The bellboy collected the remains of what had turned out to be a passable meal and started to carry them away. "I won't be but a minute, sir," he said.

The boy was as good as his word. He tapped on the door again within minutes to deliver a gallon crock, covered to keep the heat inside, which held water hot enough to steam when he poured some into the basin provided for the guests. "Anything else, sir?"

Longarm shook his head and tipped the boy a nickel for his trouble. He let the bellboy out and began to shuck his clothing.

"Reckon I'll go downstairs an' see if I can find a poker game and maybe a drink or two," he said as he kicked off his boots and dropped his britches. "I'll wash up a mite first, but don't worry. I'll leave you some water in case you want a bath too."

Actually he was not sure there was any point in talking to Lee Xua. So far the kid hadn't said one word in English, and Longarm did not know if he could understand any of it either. Still, chatter was a friendly thing even if the words were not known, so he figured it would make the boy feel better to be talked to whether he understood or not.

Longarm stripped and commenced soaking a washcloth in the hot water. Lee Xua reached in from behind—Longarm hadn't heard the kid's approach—took the wet washcloth from him, then took a two-finger dab of soft soap out of the container and lathered the cloth.

"Look," Longarm said, "I know I told you you can take a bath too, but wait till I'm done, will you please."

Lee Xua ignored the comment. Or didn't understand it. He just kept on working up a lather.

Longarm was about half pissed off. After all, what was so important that the kid had to butt in at the head of the bathing line, dammit?

Longarm was about to say something to that effect.

And then the situation got worse.

A whole helluva lot worse.

Damned if Lee Xua didn't up and start *to give Longarm a bath.*

Just started washing his chest and armpits.

Tried to anyhow.

"Hey, goddammit!" Longarm yelped, twisting away from the Chinese. "We don't . . . I mean, in this country . . . that is t' say, dammit, I don't want you giving me a bath. All right?" He backed off from the kid's touch on the double-quick and when Lee Xua followed, gave the boy a none too gentle shove in the chest to keep him away. "Don't do that no more. You hear?"

The boy heard and understood the push if not the language. His face twisted as if he felt like crying, but he didn't. After a moment he sighed and handed the washcloth back to Longarm, and Longarm went on and finished his bath. By himself.

When he was done he handed the cloth back to the kid and motioned toward the basin, miming for Lee Xua to throw out the used bathwater and pour himself some more so he could wash off too now that Longarm was done.

Lee Xua nodded, and Longarm dug into his carpetbag in search of fresh clothes for the evening.

He was paying no attention to Lee Xua, and his jaw dropped damn near to his waist when he turned and looked back at the Chinese kid again.

Lee Xua had stripped too.

And Lee Xua was a girl.

Lee Xua had tits. Tiny little saucers they were, but they were damn sure tits. Pointy little nipples, taut pale flesh with not a hint of sag or droop. Tits.

And she had a thick bush of hair as black and glossy as a raven's wing riding like a crest atop a plump little mound in the shy vee where her slim thighs almost, but not quite, came together.

What she was doing at the moment, while Longarm stood transfixed with amazement, was taking her hair down and starting to brush it out.

The braid that Longarm had taken to be a Chinese man's queue was instead merely an ordinary braid, and once let loose, her hair proved to be waist long and gleaming with good health and vitality. It was gorgeous.

And so, Longarm admitted, was Lee Xua. She was a tiny thing, slim and pretty. The face that he'd taken for that of an unshaven immature boy was now revealed to be that of a lovely girl in her late teens or perhaps her early twenties.

No wonder her cousins had wanted to keep her.

Lee Xua saw Longarm looking at her, and must have correctly assessed his expression of amazed dismay. She began to giggle and soon to openly laugh at the tall white man's consternation.

She finished brushing her hair, then daintily began to bathe from the basin of warm water.

When she was done she dropped her eyes and, naked, padded barefoot to him.

She stood before Longarm, the top of her pretty head reaching no higher than the middle of his chest. She lifted her eyes to meet his and said, "I belong you now, yes?"

"Jesus," Longarm croaked. "I almost wish you did."

Lee Xua raised herself onto her tiptoes and softly, gently began to lick and suckle Longarm's left nipple.

Chapter 18

Longarm supposed the proper thing would be to tell her to stop. Except he damn well didn't want her to.

Lee Xua had him on the bed, naked and flat on his back. For the past fifteen or twenty minutes—it felt like hours—she'd been slowly, gently, unceasingly licking and sucking on his nipples.

Longarm had had other girls nibble and lick on him before. But never quite like this. And certainly never for so long.

The thing was, the more Lee Xua did it the better it felt. The sensation ran tingling and arousing down through his belly and deep inside his groin. He could actually feel it in his balls. Which Lee Xua was also tickling and teasing, using her fingers and the softly applied ends of her fingernails. The combination was almighty fine, and at this point he could not have turned the girl away. His cock stood like a flagpole, although for the moment she was paying it no attention while she continued to suckle and slurp with the warmest, wettest, softest lips Custis Long ever in his whole life had encountered. Little Lee Xua was . . . good. Damned good.

About the time Longarm was becoming convinced that he was going to come all over himself just from the pleasures of being licked, the girl changed tactics and let her roving tongue slide south.

She licked his belly and ran her tongue inside Longarm's belly button, then continued down across his belly and onto the marble-hard pole of his cock. She smiled when she got to that landmark.

"Pretty," she murmured softly. Longarm was in no position to argue. She was indeed pretty. And if she happened to be talking about something else, well, so what. There was no harm done.

Lee Xua was as unhurried about licking his cock and his balls as she had been when she was licking Longarm's nipples. She acted as if she had the entire night to finish this. And for that matter, maybe she did. Certainly Longarm had no intention of rushing her.

She turned him onto his side so she could gently spread the cheeks of his ass, and ran her tongue around and around the rim of his asshole, then rolled him onto his back once more and . . . finally . . . commenced to suck his cock.

Lee Xua's mouth was hot on his flesh and she took him deep into her throat, holding him there for a moment while she cupped his balls in both hands so that he felt completely engulfed within the warmth of her. It was a remarkable feeling, and for that brief period of time Longarm felt as if he was detached from his body and floating free, as if the only sensations available to him were those of Lee Xua's warm, enfolding touch, as if all of him, all that was important, consisted of his penis and his testes . . . as if all of him was contained within Lee Xua's flesh.

A feeling so intense could not last for long, of course, and did not.

Before he could stop it, before he could consciously recognize what was happening, Longarm's balls released their fluids in a climax that was not an explosive burst or spasm but was, oddly and gently, a long and continuous flow of truly extraordinary pleasure.

Lee Xua grunted. And smiled a little. And accepted his semen into herself, swallowing often and then sucking again to completely empty him.

When finally she could pull no more fluid from him, she lifted her face and, smiling, turned to look at him. "You feel better now, yes?"

"Yes," he cheerfully, and accurately, agreed. He did indeed feel better now.

"Good. Make love now, okay?"

He wasn't entirely sure that he could. But if Lee Xua thought it possible, well . . . "Make love now, yes," he told her.

Lee Xua laughed and threw herself on top of him, lying on his chest with her pretty face tucked warm and small against the side of his neck. He could feel her breath there and the slight, birdlike weight of her on top of him.

When he laid a hand in the small of her back, it occurred to him that his hand felt only inches above his own belly, and he slipped his other hand between them, placing it flat against Lee Xua's stomach, with his hand on her back immediately above it. Incredibly it felt—he was quite sure of it—as if the two were literally only inches apart. Her body was so slim it seemed impossible that it could contain all the organs necessary for human survival. She was that small a girl. But she was no kid. And she damn sure knew how to please a man.

The feel of her, so small and yet so compliant, aroused him all over again, and quickly he could feel an erection grow, the massive cock swelling and pressing hard against the girl's flat, soft stomach.

Lee Xua giggled and, with a knowing twist of her hips, managed to find him and take him into her already wet receptacle.

Again Longarm felt engulfed, enveloped, completely contained within this girl's flesh.

And again he offered no protest, for this was as good as it was possible to get.

He would have to explain to her, of course, that in this country it was not proper, indeed illegal, for one human to own another, even by way of a work contract.

He would have to explain that. Of course he would.

But not now.

Later.

There would be time enough for conversation later on. And in the meantime . . .

Lee Xua began slowly, softly to move her hips.

Chapter 19

Longarm felt drained, and almighty well satisfied, as he descended the stairs into the hotel lobby. He'd left Lee Xua upstairs, naked and compliant, and he was already looking forward to returning to her. But that would have to be later. Right now there were other things he needed to think about, and personal enjoyment, no matter how good, was not one of them.

A pile of very thin newspapers on the hotel counter caught his eye, and he made a slight detour to get a better look at them. As he'd hoped, the papers proved to be copies of the special edition put out by Harry Faire's publisher friend, Anthony Morris.

Longarm laid two pennies on the counter, and took a copy of the *Fairplay Examiner* into the hotel bar with him.

A bold banner over the top of the masthead proclaimed "EXTRA! EXTRA! EXTRA!" while an only slightly smaller headline below the ornate masthead read "20,000 IN GOLD" and, in increasingly smaller sub-heads, "Kidnap and Robbery," "Huge Reward Offered," "Safe Return of Beloved Daughter Sought," "Leading Fairplay Matron Critically Wounded in Vile Attack," "Posse Mounts Rescue Attempt as Bandits Escape with Undisclosed Amount of Loot, Fairplay Bank Cleaned Out." All of which, Longarm supposed, pretty much summed up the situation, at least for the time being.

He took a seat at an only slightly soiled table and lit a cheroot. Then, tilting his head to one side and squinting to keep the rising curl of aromatic smoke out of his eyes, he commenced to read the news story Morris had hastily written earlier in the day.

Actually it wasn't a badly composed piece of work. Morris had the facts right so far as Longarm could tell. Although Longarm did think it would've been helpful had the publisher printed the names of the robbers. A man couldn't have everything, of course.

One thing that amazed the veteran deputy was the amount of loot Faire and his bankers claimed was taken. According to the story in the *Examiner,* the robbers had made off with $1,871.50.

Which sounded like a true figure.

And that, of course, was the amazement. Longarm's experience was that most bankers would claim wildly exaggerated amounts of cash when they reported robbery losses to their insurance carriers. For after all, who would be believed if the gang of bank robbers was caught and confessed to stealing a lesser amount: the asshole criminals wanting to minimize their crime, and therefore their punishment, or the fine and upstanding local citizen who'd reported the larger amount?

Harry, bless his heart, seemed not to be playing that game.

But then the robbers already knew right to the penny how much they had in hand. And Longarm supposed they would be more apt to accept the reward offer as a genuine one if they saw that the banker was being honest about the loss. Otherwise the robbers might well decide that Harry was a bigger thief than they were—a not uncommon happenstance in these affairs—and go ahead and kill the girl rather than rise to the bait of the reward.

Twenty thousand in untraceable gold—Morris's article emphasized that point several times over—was sure to be a mighty enticing lure.

The big question now, of course, would be whether the robbers learned about the reward in time to keep them from murdering Elaine Faire.

Smart crooks would go ahead and kill the girl anyway. Alive, she was and always would be a threat to them. Dead, she could tell no tales and point no fingers.

But criminals, thank goodness, were a basically stupid lot, or so Longarm had always found in the past, and twenty thousand in minted, totally untraceable gold coin was damned attractive.

For that much money a man just might take a chance. And that was Harry's only hope for the survival of his only daughter.

Longarm finished looking through the paper, tapped an inch or so of ash onto the floor, and made his way across the room to the bar. A shot of rye whiskey, or maybe two, wouldn't hurt too much.

He leaned one elbow on the bar surface and waited for the barkeep to come his way. While he was doing so the fellow standing next to him, a smallish gent with a handlebar mustache that put Longarm's to shame, tapped him lightly on the wrist.

"Is that the paper about the robbery today?" the little fellow asked.

"Ayuh."

"Could I see it for a moment, please?"

"You can have it, friend. I'm done reading it m'self."

"That's very kind of you," the man said with a smile, accepting the newspaper from Longarm.

"Tell you what, neighbor," Longarm said. "You could do me a favor in return if you would."

"Name it."

"You might could tell me if the posse's gotten back t' town."

"They have not. I know that for a fact because my business partner rode out with them. On my horse. He hasn't returned yet."

Longarm nodded. He was not surprised. But he sure would have been happy to hear that he'd figured Ed Kramer wrong and that the locals had the robber gang in custody now, and most of all, that Elaine was safe and back in her parents' hands. "What about the banker's wife. Any more news about her?" Longarm asked.

"Not that I've heard. Sorry."

Longarm shrugged. "Y'know, friend, I think you've told me more'n that paper can tell you. Can I buy you a drink by way of saying thank you?"

"That you can do," the little man said. He motioned to the barkeep, and the bartender abandoned another customer in order to respond to Longarm's companion. It would not have been polite to come right out and ask, but Longarm pretty much had to conclude that his newfound drinking partner must be a gent of some substance in the community.

The bartender brought their drinks with alacrity, and the short fellow motioned for Longarm to join him at one of the tables. He paused before taking his seat, and with a smile extended a hand to Longarm. "I'm Stan Aberdeen," he said. Which meant exactly nothing to Longarm, although from the way Aberdeen said it he obviously expected to be recognized.

Longarm introduced himself, and Aberdeen said, "I'd heard we had a federal marshal in town. You, uh, haven't looked me up in order to try and get me to invite your participation in this investigation, have you?"

"Pardon me?"

"I heard Marshal Kramer and you do not get along particularly well," Aberdeen said.

"That's true enough. But who are you that I'd ask you t' bring me in on the robbery case?"

"You don't know?"

"I sure as hell do not."

"Good," Aberdeen said. "I'm mayor of Fairplay." He smiled. "At least until the next election. And I do not need

88

to make any political enemies right now, so please don't ask me to go against the express wishes of our town marshal and one of our leading citizens. I won't do it. You should know this right off.''

Longarm shrugged. ''Mr. Mayor, I honestly had no idea who you were other than a fella that wanted t' read a newspaper. Now if you'll excuse me, I think I'm gonna wander over an' see if those boys dealin' cards in the corner want a fifth player at their table. Enjoy your drink.'' Longarm stood and politely touched the brim of his Stetson before he claimed his shot of rye off the table and carried it with him in the direction of the fellows who had themselves a poker game in progress.

''I didn't mean . . .'' Aberdeen sputtered behind him.

''It's all right, Mr. Mayor. Don't think nothing about it,'' Longarm returned without looking back nor so much as bothering to slow his pace.

Interesting, he was thinking as he walked, however. Ed Kramer wasn't even in town, being occupied with leading a posse at the moment, but the word was spreading anyway. Keep the federal man out of it. Don't nobody lend a hand to the outside lawman.

That seemed like a mighty down-deep hate, Longarm thought.

Or maybe something more.

Chapter 20

" 'Scuse me. You the marshal?"

Longarm looked up from his hand to find a whiskery, whiskey-soaked drunk peering down at him out of yellowed, rheumy eyes.

"I'm Deputy Long, yes."

"I 'uz asked t' find you, Marshal sir, an' tell you that the posse's back now an' Marshal Kramer, he wants you t' come over t' the jail." The man thought for a few moments, then added, "Please," as if he'd been specifically instructed to say that part along with the rest of the message.

"All right. Tell him I'll be right along."

"Yes, sir, thank you, sir." The rummy bobbed his head and backed away, taking a stench of sweat and whiskey breath with him.

Longarm resisted an impulse to wave a handkerchief to clear the air. "Sorry, gents. I got to leave the game now."

In truth he wasn't sorry the least little bit. The cards just weren't running his way this evening, and he considered it a stellar hand if he could so much as pair up. Queens was the best he'd drawn in the past dozen or so hands, and he was down four or five dollars for the evening. So yeah, he was pleased enough to have an excuse to get out before things got any worse.

He dropped his remaining coins into his pocket, said his good-byes, and made a quick trip up the stairs to his room to buckle on his Colt before going out to meet Kramer. Not that he'd been completely naked downstairs, but a single-shot .44-caliber derringer didn't provide much in the way of firepower, and long habit kept him from going out into the night without the big revolver. It just wouldn't have felt natural somehow.

Lee Xua smiled and pulled the sheet back to let him in beside her when Longarm first came into the room, but he told her, "Later, honey. I got work to do first." He still wasn't sure how much English the Chinese girl had, and this did not seem like the time to worry about that small detail anyway. "I won't be long."

He strapped the Colt around his waist and made sure the butt rode at the just right angle a few inches to the left of his belt buckle. Force of habit made him slide the revolver out of its leather and flick the loading gate open so he could spin the cylinder and see for himself that a fresh cartridge rested in each of five chambers. The sixth chamber was normally carried empty so the hammer could rest there and make the gun safe from accidental discharge.

Longarm closed the loading gate and started to return the double-action Colt to its holster. Then, on an impulse, he opened the gate again and thumbed a sixth cartridge into the cylinder to fully charge the big gun. He snapped the loading gate shut again and turned the cylinder manually so the striking surface of the hammer was lying on bare metal between chambers. That was semi-safe anyway. And there were times when having a sixth shot available was a helluva lot more important than passive safety.

Not that Longarm expected this evening to be such an occasion. But then, if a man always knew ahead of time

91

when trouble was coming, he likely wouldn't need to carry a gun in the first place; he could just walk wide around the trouble to begin with.

Lee Xua's eyes were big with worry when she saw him fiddling with the gun, but he gave her a smile and a reassuring kiss, then tucked the sheet high beneath her chin and told her once more that he would be back soon.

He wasn't sure that she believed him—hell, he wasn't even positive that she understood him—but she offered no protest when he left, carefully locking the door behind him so that no harm should come to the girl.

Quickly, then, he clattered down the hotel stairs and across the lobby to whatever lay in wait outside.

Chapter 21

The night air at this elevation could be bracing—even downright bitter—clean through the middle of summer, and this evening was no exception. In fact it seemed barely short of being cold when Longarm left the comfort of the hotel and ventured onto the streets of Fairplay.

He paused on the sidewalk to light a cheroot, then jammed it tight between his teeth and sank his hands into his pockets to keep the balmy air from turning them numb.

At this hour, something just short of midnight, the streets of the town were empty and all was silent, save for the far-off tinkle of a player piano that was endlessly repeating the slightly jumbled notes of a worn-out music roll.

The town provided street lamps, but most of them seemed to be burned out or blown out, or else never got lighted, because very few were alight at this hour. The little illumination that was given off by those few lamps, and by a few others left burning in store windows or whatever, picked out a still life of sunbaked ruts and windblown litter.

In the block ahead, a lanky dog with stepladder ribs and only half a tail sniffed the mouth of a narrow alley separating two buildings, then shied away as something, a cat or whatever, startled it.

The dog investigated the dark, yawning entry to Graub's Hardware, then came back out and, lifting its muzzle, scented Longarm as he approached. Nervously, tail tucked low in fear but hopeful despite that, the dog trotted down the street to meet Longarm.

"Sorry, old fellow," he muttered around the end of his cheroot. He thought about the leftovers he and the girl discarded after their meal earlier, but of course it was too late to reclaim them. He had no scraps to give the hungry animal. Pity.

The dog responded to Longarm's voice with a hesitant sweep of what little tail it possessed, then spun back the way it had come and padded along before him as if wanting to remain close. Without letting this unknown human come *too* close.

When the dog reached the mouth of the gap between buildings where it had shied before, it did more or less the same thing again, this time trembling and darting swiftly back away from the dark alley.

Longarm frowned. And took two quick steps to his left, ducking into the recess at the entry to the hardware.

A sheet of yellow flame briefly turned night into day on that small stretch of sidewalk, and an ear-splitting roar shattered the peace of the night.

Somewhere down the street Longarm could hear shotgun pellets rattling like hail as they harmlessly thumped into earth and wood.

Somewhere inside the narrow alley he could hear the muffled thud of running footsteps as the would-be assassin turned and ran.

Longarm leaped forward, throwing himself into the alley behind the gunman. It occurred to him just a tad too late to question whether there might be *two* ambushers, not one, and whether they might be pretty sharp hombres after all.

Luckily, there was only the one. One dumb one.

The gunman wasn't halfway down the alley by the time Longarm broke into the clear there. And the man was in sharp silhouette against the dull yellow light spill of a lantern burning outside somebody's two-hole crapper.

Longarm could scarcely believe anyone could have been stupid enough to choose that particular alley, with a steady light behind it, for an ambush site.

But then the everlasting stupidity of crooks, cons, and other criminals was one of the few verities that a peace officer could rely upon.

Longarm palmed his Colt and took careful aim.

"Halt. Or I'll shoot."

He didn't wait for an answer. Hell, there was no point in that. Not only had he never seen it, he'd never so much as *heard* of a fleeing killer who actually *obeyed* that time-honored order.

So after he shouted the words that Marshal Billy Vail liked his deputies to shout at times like these, he lowered his aim a mite and triggered a slug into the back of the running man's legs, just a few inches south of his butt.

The guy went down practically before Longarm fired, dropping like a partridge with a load of Number Five shot up its ass.

"Don't move. Not an inch," Longarm warned. "I can still see you clear."

Which was, in fact, a lie. Once the fellow fell onto the ground, he was no longer in silhouette and was completely lost to view from Longarm's end of the alley, lying amid the discarded cans and smashed crates and other oddments of jetsam, flotsam, or similar shit that littered the infrequently traveled alleyway. He could have been lying there knitting socks or loading shotguns. Longarm couldn't see to know the difference. The best Longarm could do was hope the son of a bitch was doing what he was told, and edge forward with his ears tuned in readiness for the sound of a shotgun hammer being cocked. And duck pretty damn quick if he heard one.

Slowly and carefully, he edged deeper into the alley.

It took him a cautious three minutes or so to reach the man he'd shot.

That was mostly time wasted.

Once he got to the fellow, he could see that not all was what he'd expected.

Oh, he'd hit the guy, all right.

And his bullet had surely gone where he'd pointed it.

It was just that when the fellow had seemed to go down too quickly, that was because he had.

Apparently the man had tripped—there was a broken keg in the alley that was a likely culprit—and started to fall an instant or so before Longarm fired.

Because of that, or whatever other reason there might have been, Longarm's slug had not found the meat of the man's thigh as Longarm had intended. Instead the bullet had made a neat hole in the back of the man's skull where it went in. And a very messy one just above the bridge of his nose where it came out again.

It was the sort of wound that would make a squeamish man puke.

Longarm only grunted. And if he could taste a hint of bile in the back of his throat, well, the mellow flavor of good cigar smoke would cover that without overmuch bother.

Longarm wasn't sure, but he stepped over the corpse and went over to the outhouse to fetch down the lantern that was burning there. He carried it back and used its light to more closely examine the body of the man he'd just killed. Most of the face was intact. Distorted some, but essentially in place. The dead man, the man who'd tried to kill Longarm, was the same shabby rummy who'd come to the hotel saloon and asked Longarm to meet Ed Kramer at the jail.

Scowling, Longarm knelt beside the dead man and began rifling his pockets.

He was busily engaged in that task when he heard the clack of a gun hammer being cocked. The sound came from the street end of the alley, from where Longarm himself had been just minutes earlier when he shot the oh-so-nicely silhouetted ambusher.

"Hold it there, mister. Don't move," a nervously squeaking voice ordered. "Don't you move or I'll blow your belly out your backbone." The words were brave enough, but the speaker sounded almighty young and almighty frightened, and Longarm was half afraid the kid might do by accident what he probably couldn't do on purpose.

"Stand easy, friend," Longarm said softly. "I'll be still as a pigeon-shit statue. Just don't shoot without cause, okay?"

Longarm turned his head slowly around.

And for the second time within the span of mere minutes found himself on the wrong end of a pair of scattergun muzzles.

Chapter 22

"Easy now," Longarm said, his hands spread wide and held in plain sight. "I'm a deputy U.S. marshal. This here fella—"

"Shut your damn mouth," the man with the shotgun said. Helluva rude thing to do, interrupting a man when he's trying to tell you something.

"But I only—"

"You keep on talking, mister, and I'll blow a hole through your belly big enough you can crawl inside and hide there." The words were brave enough but there was something in the timbre of the man's voice, a hint of quaver, a smattering of hesitation, that made Longarm suspect this fellow was scared about half to death himself, never mind the effect he was having on Longarm.

And if there was anything a man ought to be purely afraid of, at least in Custis Long's opinion, it was a fella who had a case of nerves. His own fear could make him yank the trigger without ever meaning to do it. Hell, Longarm had seen men get so jittery and out of sorts that their trembling set off a trigger. Accidental death, of course. But you'd be every speck as dead once the deed was done as from a shooting done on purpose.

The man with the shotgun stood there for long, silent moments while Longarm continued to kneel beside the dead man, illuminated in complete detail by the lantern he'd set down beside the body. Unfortunately.

After a bit it became apparent that the townie—who almost had to be one of Ed Kramer's deputies—had no idea what to do with this varmint that he'd gone and captured. He had Longarm cold. But now what?

Longarm shifted his weight slightly, and the cartilage in his right knee crackled like dry kindling being broken ready for the fire.

"Can I move, please?" he asked. "My leg is goin' to sleep an' I'm afraid if I fall over you'll shoot." That was a lie but what the hell, the Fairplay lawman couldn't know it.

"Keep your hands out where I can see them. You can stand up now."

Longarm nodded and slowly, very slowly, came to his feet. The other knee popped too.

"I really am a federal deputy," Longarm said softly. "This man tried to ambush me. Him and his shotgun, you can see it right there, was the first noise you would've heard. My fire was the next."

"Down the length of a dark alley in the middle of the night and hit him right in the head. That's pretty fancy shooting, don't you think?"

"Too fancy t' believe, I agree with you, friend, but I didn't try an' hit him there. An' no, I wasn't standing right behind him to shoot him deliberate like that. I aimed lower. He tripped an' dropped into the bullet. An' you can believe that or shove it up your ass, it don't make no nevermind t' me." Longarm had had about enough of this youngster. And anyway, now that they were talking, it seemed improbable that the fellow would shoot. That made for a pretty good theory anyhow.

"How do I know you're who you say you are?" the townie asked.

"I got a wallet with a badge in it just inside my coat here. You want me to reach for it or would you rather fish it out yourself?"

"I'll get it." The local sidled closer, so close he could not possibly have swung the shotgun around to bear even if Longarm had a trick up his sleeve. He reached inside Longarm's coat and felt around for the pocket and wallet there.

While he was busy doing that, Longarm probably didn't have more than six or eight opportunities to snatch the shotgun away from him.

But no matter how much the young fellow needed the learning experience that would have given him, it would have been nothing but a grandstand play. And besides, tomfoolishness like that too often led to accidents. Longarm had no more desire to be killed by accident than he did by design, so he stood meek and cooperative as any lamb and let the deputy frisk him unmolested.

The local deputy—Longarm could see the glint of a cheap badge on his shirt now that he was closer to the lantern light—took his eyes off his prisoner while he examined the contents of Longarm's wallet. Again, there probably were not more than a handful of times when Longarm could have used that as a chance to take his shotgun away and bust it over his skull.

"You really *are* the federal man that Marshal Kramer can't abide," the fellow said.

"That's me, all right." Longarm introduced himself more properly, and the townie lowered the muzzles of his shotgun and let the hammers down to safe cock.

"I'm Rodney Dewell," the townie said, rather sheepishly extending his hand for a shake. "I'm night deputy here."

Longarm explained his involvement with the dead man, then asked, "Is the posse *really* back?" He was already sure of the answer, but felt he should ask anyway.

"No, sir," Dewell told him. "We haven't had any word

from them since they rode out this morning.''

Longarm grunted. It wasn't exactly a surprise. "If you don't mind, Rod, I'll finish what I was doing there.''

"Forgive me for saying so, but it looked to me like, well . . .''

"Like I'd just backshot the man an' was busy robbing him,'' Longarm helpfully finished. "O' course it did. But what I was doin', Rod, was looking to see was there anything on the man that would tell me who hired him t' kill me.''

"Hired him? Why would somebody do that?''

"Damned if I know. But I'd sure like to find out, an' knowing who might be a leg up on findin' out why.''

"Oh. Sure.'' Dewell bobbed his head. "I can see how that would be.''

"Hold the light for me an' we'll finish finding out what this dead man can tell us.''

Night Marshal Rodney Dewell looked more than a trifle squeamish about that idea, but he dutifully bent to retrieve the lantern, and held it while Longarm resumed rifling the person of the dead man.

Chapter 23

Longarm sat on the edge of the bed and pulled his left boot off, leaning down to set it gently on the floor rather than allowing it to fall as he ordinarily would. Lee Xua was sound asleep on the wall side of the bed, peaceful as a babe and pretty as a picture. Her black hair spread over the pillow like a glossy fan, picking up the light of the lamp she'd left burning for him and reflecting the gleam of the flame in softly curling waves.

He took his other boot off and removed his socks, then stood to shuck the rest of his clothes.

His mind was active while he performed those routine chores. He kept trying to gain a clear picture that would help lead him to whoever it was who'd hired the dead rummy this evening. And why.

Dammit, there was no one in Fairplay, not even Harry, or perhaps especially not Harry, who should feel so strongly about Longarm's presence as to hire a killer. Not even a miserably inept one like . . . what had Rodney Dewell called him? Mac something. No, it was something-or-other Mac. Whiskey Mac, that was it. A nickname or a part of a name, no more than that. The man's proper identification seemed to be unknown here, and unless someone came forward to tell the straight of it, the man who was called Whiskey Mac would be buried with only that and perhaps the date of his death carved onto a cheap wooden marker. In a few years that would rot away and be gone, and there would be nothing at all left behind to mark the deadbeat's passage through this life.

It seemed a shitty enough way for a man to reach his end. But then perhaps Whiskey Mac deserved no more. He seemed to have given little enough to the world he inhabited, so perhaps it was only fitting that he take nothing beyond it, not even his own name.

And he'd left damn little behind, that was for sure. Not even any clues to who it was who'd hired him on this, his last night of life.

When Longarm went through Whiskey Mac's pockets he found scant pickings. A rusting penknife with one of its two blades broken off. A bandanna stiff with dried snot. Three pennies. And five bright and shiny new ten-dollar gold eagles.

"Fifty dollars in gold?" Rodney Dewell gasped when Longarm showed him the coins spread out in the palm of his hand to catch the lantern light. "I wouldn't think old Mac would've seen fifty dollars in gold for this whole year past. For sure not all at one time, and likely not if you added up everything that passed through his hands during that time. Hell, mister, everything he got hold of he spent on whiskey, just as quick as he could make it to the nearest saloon. With fifty dollars all at one time, old Mac would've drunk himself to death inside a week. Hell, inside two days. He would've tried to drink it all up in one blowout and that would've been the end of him."

Which, Longarm reflected now, might have been part of the idea when someone hired the old rummy. Get him to do the job. After all, nobody could miss if he had a close range and a shotgun in his hands, could he? And then let him drink himself to death afterward.

And if the man babbled in his liquor while he was engaged in that process of self-destruction, well, who paid any attention to smelly old rummies anyhow. Folks never listened to them, much less believed them.

Fifty dollars.

Longarm smiled to himself as he leaned down to blow the lamp out, then slipped beneath the sheet that was covering Lee Xua's slim and perfect little body.

Fifty dollars.

It seemed kind of insulting.

Killing a fella of Longarm's professional standing surely ought to be worth more than a lousy fifty dollars.

Why, now that he thought about it, he felt downright miffed.

First chance he got, dammit, he would have to have some strong words for whoever it was that hired Whiskey Mac.

Yessir, he would have to explain to that jehu the error of his ways.

A deputy marshal of Custis Long's experience and ability should be worth at least . . . what? A thousand dollars gold? A hundred? Fifty-*five* bucks anyway.

Sure he should. Longarm pulled the sheet up underneath his chin, and tried not to think about the girl whose breathing was soft and sweet in his ear.

Chapter 24

He felt her hand first, gliding across the flat planes of his belly as lightly as a spider's nocturnal march. Her hand, then her breath warm on his chest, finally the moist warmth as her tongue found and began gently to tease and titillate his right nipple.

Longarm had no idea what time it was. Sometime in the middle of the night. That was as close as he could measure it.

Whenever it was now, Lee Xua was awake. Playfully awake. And almighty artful at what she was doing, which, at the moment, was to busy herself with Longarm's arousal.

Oh, she was doing a fine job of that.

She licked and suckled his nipple while one small hand sought out his balls to cup and warm them and then to toy with them.

Longarm felt his cock stir from its slumber and begin to stiffen, and Lee Xua, feeling the response, smiled and murmured something in her own language.

She sat up then, pushing the sheet off Longarm's lean body.

A faint silver glow of mingled light from street lamps, moon, and stars filtered through the thin muslin curtain over the hotel room window. The light was enough to give Longarm a dim but enticing view of Lee Xua's slim pale form as she shifted position over him.

She appeared no bigger around than a cattail reed, but there was beauty in her tiny body. And a resilient strength that he would not have suspected.

Lee Xua knelt above him and let her hair, loose now and brushed out to a smooth glossy sheen, fall onto his skin. The feel of it was cool and so light, he might almost have believed he was imagining the faint sensations, except that he could see the dark spread of it where it so lightly touched his body.

The girl swayed back and forth over him, dragging the tips of her hair over his face and neck, down onto his nipples, lower to his belly, and finally onto his stiff cock and throbbing balls.

He reached out to place a hand in the small of her back, and felt the thin veneer of flesh that covered the sharp bones of her spine. The feel of her skin was taut and tender and very exciting to him.

For agonizingly long moments she moved above him, sweeping the tip ends of her hair over him quite literally from head to toe and back again, but with generous stopovers in the middle that nearly drove him crazy.

When he was sure he could take no more of that, when he ached to reach down and grab her and slam her lovely face down onto his erection, Lee Xua dipped her head and resumed using her tongue on him. His ears, his throat, his nipples. She licked his belly and probed his belly button with the tip of her tongue. She sucked his balls and licked the exquisitely sensitive expanse of flesh that lay between his testicles and his asshole. And finally she took him deep into her mouth.

By then Longarm was soaring so high he was ready to explode at the least touch.

Lee Xua seemed to sense this, for she took him into her mouth only briefly, for a few seconds and no more. When she pulled away, she deliberately left him moist with her spittle so the night air was chill on the head of his cock, and the danger of an early ejaculation subsided.

Without pausing to allow him to rest, Lee Xua swung one slender leg over his waist, poising above him and reaching down to find his shaft and guide its head to the gates of her pleasure.

She was already wet from the excitement of arousing Longarm, he discovered. She was already set to receive him.

With a gasp of obvious joy, Lee Xua allowed her hips to sink, guiding him into the wet folds of her small body.

Tiny though she was, she gleefully took all of him into herself, spearing her tight, moist vagina on Longarm's strong shaft.

Lee Xua gasped again and stiffened, then after little more than a heartbeat of time, relaxed and began, slowly at first, but then with growing speed and intensity, to bounce and grind atop him, jabbing his pole harder and deeper into her body with each passing moment until she was leaping and convulsing at a frantic pace.

Longarm held back as long as he could, longer than he would have thought humanly possible. He was rewarded with a sharp outcry that ripped from Lee Xua's throat as she reached a climax mere seconds before the dam burst and Longarm's juices spewed hot and thick into the girl.

He shuddered as wave after wave of heavy aftershocks rocked him.

Lee Xua went stiff in her own passionate throes. Then, like a marionette whose paddles had been dropped, she collapsed onto him, so slim and small that he scarcely felt the weight of her.

Longarm's breathing slowed eventually, and he could feel her heartbeat soft against his flesh as she lay atop him.

He left her there, not wanting to disturb the deep sleep of utter satiation that had claimed her, and while he wanted a midnight cheroot now, he wanted more to reward the

107

sweet Chinese girl for the joy she brought to him, and so he let her sleep on, using his chest and belly to rest on.

And while he lay awake in the night waiting for his own return to sleep, he thought about Janet lying in pain beyond his imagining, and he wondered what the morrow would bring to her, to Harry, to the girl child the two of them both loved.

Chapter 25

The girl sat with her eyes down, her hands folded delicately in lap. She looked embarrassed, Longarm thought, and with damned good reason. They'd been sitting in the hotel restaurant for eight, ten minutes now, and hadn't so much as attracted the notice of one of the waiters.

At least not that any of them would admit to. The plain truth, of course, was that as a Chinese, Lee Xua was not welcome here. The folks at the hotel would be thinking that she should go eat among her own kind. Longarm understood the attitude. Didn't share it, but did comprehend it. And so, obviously, did Lee Xua.

Regardless of that, however, as long as the girl was in his company she would be treated like a lady. Well, in public, anyhow. Never mind how the two of them might get along in private. The point was, she was with him now, and the waiters were ignoring him as much as they were ignoring the girl. Longarm wasn't much inclined to put up with that bullshit.

"Excuse me," he said, folding his napkin and laying it beside his as yet unused silverware. "I gotta go see if I can borrow a match." He gave Lee Xua a smile and stood, pulling a cheroot out of his pocket as an excuse to leave the table.

"Excuse me," he said again as he buttonholed one of the dining room waiters and, smiling, drew the man off to the side of the big room.

"Yes, sir?" The waiter, the largest and most burly of those on duty at the moment, cast a skeptical look in Lee Xua's direction even while he was speaking to Longarm.

"You know who I am," Longarm suggested.

"Yes, sir," the waiter affirmed.

"What you don't know, friend, is that I can be one notional son of a bitch."

"I wouldn't know about—"

"Quiet," Longarm ordered in a calm, no-nonsense tone. "Sir?"

"What I am sayin', friend, is that you'd best hush your mouth for a minute while you listen to me."

The waiter sneered. "If you think I'm going to lower myself to waiting on some Celestial slut like—"

"Now that is the exact sort of thing that can get a man in trouble," Longarm said in a deceptively pleasant tone before the man could finish.

"My boss won't—"

Again Longarm cut the words short. "Your boss won't be able to do shit about the things I personally will have done to you by that time, my friend."

"I don't see what you think you can—"

"Friend, d'you think I picked you because you were handy? I chose you, old son, because you're the biggest an' the meanest-looking o' the bunch that's working here this morning. Can you think why I might've wanted t' do that? No? I'll tell you. I don't want nobody, not you, not the management, not those other waiters, to think that I'll back off. Not a lick, I won't. An' to prove it, friend, I'm downright willing to waste this here fine cigar by first lighting it an' then seeing how far I can put the coal end up

110

your fat nose. After which I will prob'ly break something. You right-handed? Fine. How'd you like each finger on your right hand busted. You think I can't do it? You think I won't?''

"I, uh . . ."

Longarm smiled and patted the waiter on the shoulder. Anyone observing the two of them but out of hearing, which would include anyone else in the dining room, since Longarm's voice was calm and low, would surely have thought the two men were having a friendly chat.

"It won't take me but a minute." Longarm smiled again. "Be no trouble at all, believe me."

The waiter's eyes hardened and he took a deep breath. For a moment Longarm thought the fellow was a braver man than Longarm had given him credit for.

The man looked past Longarm, to Lee Xua probably, and then back again. He swallowed as he seemed to think about the threat.

"Go ahead," Longarm invited. "Try me." He pulled a match out and lit the cheroot, deliberately sending a stream of aromatic smoke into the waiter's face.

The waiter coughed. And his pose of bravado was broken. "You want . . ."

"Ham, eggs, hotcakes, the usual thing. For two, if you please. Oh, yes, an' tea for the lady, coffee for me. Don't forget to bring out some tea that's nice an' hot. You hear me, friend?''

"I, um . . . yes, sir."

"Thank you very much. Nice talkin' to you." Longarm smiled and patted the waiter's shoulder again, then turned and went back to the table where Lee Xua waited. "I went ahead an' ordered for both of us while I had his attention." Longarm gave the girl a smile too, then unfolded his napkin and laid it over his lap.

The waiter was there within seconds, bearing coffee for Longarm. And fresh, steaming hot tea for the Chinese girl.

Breakfast turned out to be a pretty good meal after all.

When they were done eating, Longarm took Lee Xua up to the room and told her to wait there for him. Then he took his Winchester and saddle scabbard and headed for the livery stable where big old George waited.

"You can have him again today if you like," the hostler told him, "but I have a better saddle horse available now if you'd rather."

"How's that?" Longarm asked around the stub of his after-meal cigar.

"Fellow came in last night off the posse. He turned the horse back in and didn't say anything about needing it again today, so you can have him if you want."

"I want," Longarm said without even asking about the animal. Whatever it was, it had to be better than poor old George. "But who is this guy that was out with the posse? Did he say anything about their progress?"

"Not to me, he didn't. He was tired and I was half asleep. All I know is what I've already told you," the livery operator said. "As for who he is, he's one of our town deputies. Horace Marts by name."

"Tell you what," Longarm said, tossing the butt of his cheroot down and carefully crushing it to make sure no live coal could be windblown into the hay or the highly flammable straw in and around the stable. "Go ahead an' get that horse tacked up an' ready for me if you would, please. I want t' go see if I can find this Marts fella and have a word with him before I ride out."

"Sure, I can do that. Hand me that carbine, and I'll hang it on the saddle for you if you want."

"I appreciate that, but I'll carry it with me," Longarm said politely. It wasn't that he did not trust the hostler. Exactly.

It was more that he did not trust *anyone,* anyone short of Billy Vail that is, to handle Longarm's weapons, especially out of Longarm's own sight.

A man might need a gun without warning, and if someone else had been fooling with the thing, there might still be a cartridge in the chamber when one was needed. Or there might not.

Worse, and never mind how improbable, a stranger could

very well break a firing pin, say, by accident or on purpose, or do something equally destructive.

Longarm simply felt better knowing his weapons were safe in his own hands. "Go ahead an' get the horse ready, if you please. I won't be long."

The hostler nodded and spat a stream of dark tobacco juice, barely missing a dung beetle that crawled slowly on. "It will be ready when you are," he promised as Longarm headed for the Fairplay jail.

Chapter 26

Horace Marts was in his early twenties or thereabouts. He did not much look like Longarm's idea of a deputy marshal. He was short and lightly built and wore spectacles. Not that that should be held against him, of course, as you couldn't really tell just from looking. Billy Vail's chief clerk Henry was lightly built and wore spectacles, and he had as much grit as a hungry bulldog.

Still, there was something about Marts, an undefinable sense or impression that he gave off, that Longarm distrusted.

And no, that wasn't exactly right either. Quite probably the young man was as honest and trustworthy as a Regulator clock. It was just that Longarm suspected he was not . . . effective. As a lawman. Nice fella, maybe. But not hard enough for this job.

For instance, he looked positively embarrassed and uncertain about what to do when Longarm introduced himself. It was entirely obvious that he, like practically everyone else in Fairplay, knew that Ed Kramer and Custis Long were on the outs.

But instead of taking a stand on his boss's side, which Longarm would have fully understood, Deputy Marts hemmed and hawed and then nervously offered the visiting U.S. deputy a seat. Longarm would have had more respect for the young man if he'd been sullen and stubborn and made the visitor remain standing.

Longarm suspected young Horace was one of those people who just couldn't stand to have anyone, not even the criminals they were arresting, take a dislike to them. That sort wanted the world to be all sweetness and light. Which it just plain wasn't.

Longarm accepted the offered chair, however, and leaned back to cross his legs and give Marts a smile. "I came by hoping to hear that the posse is doing some good out there," Longarm said.

Marts shrugged. "We, uh, that is to say they, they didn't find much."

"Tracks? Sightings? Anything at all?"

"Well, um, not really. We stopped and talked to everybody we came across, but nobody was able to tell us anything useful. The marshal, he said they'll ride cross-country today down toward Kenosha Pass and see has anybody down that way seen the gang. Or Elaine, of course. She's our biggest worry." From the way Marts blushed slightly when he added that last part, Longarm suspected the deputy had something of a personal interest in finding Elaine Faire. Not that there was necessarily anything between the two of them. But Longarm guessed that Horace Marts wished there might someday be.

"Cold camp last night?" Longarm asked.

"Oh, no, not at all. We doubled back to Alma and put up there. There wasn't room enough for everybody at the hotel, so some of the gents slept in the hayloft at the livery stable there." Marts frowned a little. "It's a funny thing, but the gentlemen who volunteered to do that weren't at all the ones I would've thought would be willing to rough it.

I mean, they were real gentlemen, not the young men at all.''

Overaged boys having fun and proving to each other—to themselves most of all—that they were still tough and capable. Longarm thought that, but refrained from saying anything. No point to it.

''Why did you come back in the night like that, Horace?'' Longarm asked.

''The marshal told me to, of course. I wouldn't have left them if . . .''

''I hadn't meant anything like that, son. O' course I didn't,'' Longarm assured him. ''It just kinda surprised me that the marshal would have reduced the size of his posse like that.''

''It was for a good reason, sir,'' Marts said. ''The marshal wanted some notes brought back to town. He said I was to be his . . . courier, that's the word he used. I was his courier last night.''

''Notes?''

''Yes, sir. For the mayor, for Elaine's father, one or two others. I don't know what Marshal Kramer said in those notes anyway, and even if I did I don't know that I ought to tell.''

''I wouldn't ask you something like that,'' Longarm said quickly. He wasn't sure just how far he meant it. But it sounded nice and couldn't hurt, since the deputy said he didn't know to begin with.

''Yes, sir. Well, anyhow, he wrote out the notes after everybody got settled into the hotel, and he gave them to me and told me to fetch them back. Which is why I'm down here now. Can I ask you something?''

''Sure.''

''Did you really . . . I mean . . . did you shoot somebody last night?''

''That was me.''

Marts shivered. He looked a mite pale. ''Rod Dewell left a note about that, but I wasn't sure.''

''He tried to shoot me first,'' Longarm said.

"I've never been shot at," Marts offered. "I hope to God I never am."

"Are you sure you're in the right line o' work, son?"

"People respect a deputy," Marts responded uneasily.

"An' they show that respect by buying their deputies real nice coffins when a fellow turns out t' not quite have what it takes," Longarm suggested.

"Don't say that. Please."

"Sorry." But he wasn't. He hoped Marts reconsidered his choice of employment, maybe took up bartending or clerking in a store, something like that.

Not that it was any of his business.

"You say you took a message to Mr. Faire?"

"That's right."

"Any word lately on how Mrs. Faire is doing?"

Marts shook his head. "I stopped by there again this morning on my way in. The doctor was with her, but the lady I spoke with said there hadn't been any change in the night. She said Mrs. Faire never got any sleep."

"No, I wouldn't expect so." Longarm sighed and lifted himself to his feet, replacing the flat-crowned Stetson on his head and stifling a yawn. He hadn't gotten much sleep last night either, although not for the same reason as poor, dying Janet. "Thanks for your help, Deputy."

"Yes, uh, yes, sir. Will you, um, be riding out to join the posse, Marshal?"

"No, I don't think your boss would want me interfering. I'm just concerned, that's all. The Faires are old friends of mine. We sorta grew up together back a long time ago."

Marts looked considerably relieved by that news. "I didn't know that, sir."

"Old friends," Longarm repeated lamely to himself, his voice small and hushed as a sense of helplessness swept through him. Poor Janet. Poor Harry. Worst of all was that poor child of theirs. "If you hear anything more . . ." He let the words trail away. If Marts heard anything more, what? He damn sure wouldn't come running to Longarm with it. Not the way Marts's own boss felt about the federal deputy. And Longarm couldn't reasonably ask him to. "I, uh, I'll stop by again now an' then if you don't mind.''

"Yes, sir. Whatever you say.''

Longarm frowned and left the city jail, his pace lengthening as he strode back to the livery.

Not that he expected to accomplish anything by flailing around in the woods. But he had to do *something* even if there was nothing constructive he could contribute to the situation.

He couldn't stand to simply sit around and wait. He simply could not.

Chapter 27

Longarm put plenty of miles on the rented horse, but that was all he was able to accomplish. If, that is, one could count that as an accomplishment.

He examined countless hoofprints and footpaths, talked to every human he could find in an arc that ranged from the upper reaches of Trout Creek Pass all the way around past Hartsel and beyond the road to Bailey and Tarryall.

Fairplay Marshal Ed Kramer and his posse apparently were covering the approaches from—or quick exits to—Kenosha and Hoosier Passes, at least according to what Horace Marts had said.

As far as Longarm could determine then, pretty much the full range of possible escape routes had been looked at either by the posse or by Longarm in person.

Yet no one, absolutely no one, seemed to have seen the bank robbers, the kidnapped girl, or anyone remotely resembling any of them.

It was frustrating, Longarm admitted to himself as he rode wearily back into town.

He dismounted outside the livery stable and whistled to let the hostler know he was there.

The liveryman came out to take charge of his horse, and Longarm reclaimed his scabbard and Winchester from the saddle, then started back toward the hotel at a slow and dispirited gait.

Reluctant to hear the news, but unable to avoid the inevitable truth, he stopped first at the Faire house, where once more there was a dragon guarding the gate in the form of an elderly female.

"What is your name, young man?" the biddy demanded with an audible sniff and a stare of critical suspicion.

Young man. Longarm kinda liked that. It was not something he heard all that often anymore. He admitted to his identity.

"I thought as much. She's been asking for you, God only knows why. The mister said if you showed up you should go upstairs and look in on her. But mind now, if she's sleeping, you're not to wake her. You can wait for her to wake on her own, or you can come back later. But don't you dare wake her. And I will thank you to leave that . . . thing"—she gave the Winchester a look that would have melted the weapon had its steel not been properly tempered—"in the vestibule. I doubt you will need it inside here."

"Yes, ma'am," Longarm said meekly. He hadn't been willing to leave the carbine with the man at the livery earlier. The same caution would not apply here. Besides, he was sure the Winchester would be as safe under the old bag's suspicious eyes as if it had been locked inside Harry Faire's bank vault.

No, on second thought, and considering recent events, he was sure the Winchester was *safer* here than it would have been in the vault. Robbers could break open an ordinary bank vault, but Longarm didn't know of any power on earth that could stand up to the deadly gaze of a gray-haired biddy like this one.

Longarm removed his Stetson and left both the hat and the rifle scabbard on the hat rack beside the front door. Then he took the stairs two at a time on his way up to answer Janet's summons.

"She's sleeping," the gate dragon's twin sister, or some reasonable facsimile thereof, told him outside Janet's bedroom door. What the woman almost certainly meant was that Janet had been drugged, perhaps without her knowledge, to give her some ease from the horrible pains that came with a stomach wound. Still and all, whether genuinely asleep or in a drug-induced stupor, the effect would be the same. Janet was out of touch for the time being.

Longarm gnawed at the ends of his mustache. He was tired; he was dirty; he was hungry; he had a thousand things that he probably ought to be doing. But Janet had asked for him. She was dying and in pain and she had asked for him. He couldn't just walk away now to wait for a more convenient time to call upon her.

"I'll wait," he said.

"There is a chair in the next room there. You can bring it and join me," the volunteer nurse—friend or neighbor or church member or whatever—told him.

Longarm carried the suggested chair into Janet's bedroom, which was dark and smelled of medicines. He settled quietly into a corner and sat there with as much patience as he could muster while the nurse just as silently sat tatting a lacy something-or-other. Longarm wished he had something like that to occupy his hands.

Instead he found his mind occupied. With thoughts of Janet back when they were young. Back when they were both kids and she was so crazy in love with him. Back when she'd been so generous with the delights of her young and exciting body.

How would it have been—for the both of them—if he'd gone back to her once the fighting was done? Different, yes. Of course. But . . . better?

That was not for him to know. It never would be.

He closed his eyes and tried to think about other things.

About Janet's daughter, who he'd never seen. About little Lee Xua waiting for him back at the hotel. About Harry Faire and the success Harry had made of himself through these long years past. About how things might have been if he'd chosen a different path back then and if . . . no. He had to quit thinking about that.

The "what if" game was one of the roads that led to madness. Dammit, he *knew* that.

He squeezed his eyes shut tighter, and tried again to think about something distracting.

Wondered what would have happened if . . .

No!

Longarm writhed in the chair as if in physical agony and breathed, "God, please," half under his breath. He himself did not know if the softly whispered words were a complaint or a prayer.

Chapter 28

Janet was still unconscious or asleep, and Longarm himself was close to dropping off into a snooze, when the door slammed open with a bang, and Harry Faire came bursting in with Ed Kramer on his heels. Their entrance was so loud and unexpected that Longarm sprang onto his feet and had his Colt halfway out of the holster before he realized there was no need for alarm.

"What the hell are you doing here?" Kramer immediately demanded.

Ahead of the town marshal, though, Harry Faire was ignoring Kramer, Longarm, and everything else while he rushed to his wife's bedside. "Wake up, Janet. You have to hear this."

He touched her shoulder lightly and when that did no good, shook her just a little.

That—the movement must have been excruciating because it lanced clean through whatever soporific the dying woman had been given earlier—brought her around.

Janet's eyes came open, and despite the horrible pain she must have been experiencing, she never winced. "Sweetheart?" she whispered.

Harry dropped to his knees at her side and took her hand tenderly into both of his. He leaned down, grinning, to kiss the hand he was holding, then in a voice choked with joyful emotion said, "She's still alive, darling. Elaine is alive. We've heard from the robbers. They know about our reward offer. They say they will exchange her for gold."

Janet began to cry. But by then so was Harry. Hell, Longarm could almost have joined in himself. The girl was alive. That was the thing. The robbers had heard about the reward in time and the girl was alive.

Longarm came closer, not wanting to miss overhearing a single syllable. On the other side of the bed Ed Kramer was doing the same thing.

"They sent a note," Harry was explaining to his wife. "They sent a note, dear, saying Elaine is safe and well and that they will contact us again soon to tell us how they want to handle the exchange. Isn't that wonderful, darling? Isn't that just about the finest thing you've ever heard?" Harry's tears were flowing freely now, and he was smiling as he clung tight to Janet's delicate hand.

Janet was able to give him a wan smile. Then her eyes drooped shut and she allowed the medication once more to claim her.

Harry stayed with her for some minutes, but Janet was deep in slumber now. Eventually he stood and, motioning for Kramer to follow, tiptoed out of the shuttered and heavily draped sickroom.

Longarm hesitated only for a moment. Then he too slipped silently out into the hallway and followed the men downstairs.

He wanted to learn more about this message the robber gang was said to have sent.

It was only later that he realized he had not yet had a chance to speak with Janet and learn what it was she'd wanted to say to him when she'd asked that he come to her.

Chapter 29

"D'you think I could—"

"Get the hell outa here," Ed Kramer snapped.

Longarm looked to Harry for a response. After all, it was Harry's place.

Longarm had followed the two of them downstairs and into what proved to be a handsomely furnished study just off the foyer. The study reflected Harry Faire's wealth and his taste. No deer heads or cow horns here, thank you. Instead it was furnished in polished mahogany and gold brocade. Prints of hunt scenes—the horse-riding kind with red coats and hounds—decorated the walls, and over the massive fireplace hung an oil portrait of a slightly younger Janet along with a pretty little girl of twelve or so in ruffles and flounces. The child would be Elaine, of course. She looked very young in the painting, but sweet. Longarm had never seen Harry and Janet's child, but for some reason he almost had the impression that he should know her, that she should be familiar to him. Once the painting caught his eye, he couldn't quit looking at it.

"Get the hell out of here, I said," Kramer repeated.

Longarm quit staring at the portrait. Janet was so beautiful he could scarcely believe it, and he wondered anew why he'd ever stayed away those long years back. Then he looked first at Kramer, and back again to Harry.

"You heard him, Custis," Harry said.

"But Harry, I—"

"No, Custis. Not here. Ed is in charge now, and he doesn't want you involved. I promised him I would—"

"Dammit, Harry, d'you want me to beg you? All right, I'm begging. Tell me what's going on. Tell me what you've heard."

"I want you to leave now, Custis," Harry Faire said in a voice that seemed tinged with sadness despite being firm and uncompromising.

"I can't believe—"

"Get out, damn you, or I'll have you arrested," Kramer snarled. The man sounded almighty eager to arrange for exactly that to happen, Longarm thought. Although if it came down to it, it would require Kramer and every damned deputy he . . . no, Longarm acknowledged with a sigh. If it came down to that Longarm would be obligated to keep his mouth shut and let himself be hauled away. He couldn't do otherwise and still claim any respect for the law. Or for himself. But this was one bitter sonuvabitch of a pill to have to swallow.

"You're making a mistake, Harry," Longarm protested weakly.

"Get out," Kramer said. "I won't tell you again."

Longarm gave the portrait over the mantle one last long look. Then he turned and left.

"Miz Marts?" Longarm removed his Stetson and held it in both hands. He was doing his best to look meek and polite and inoffensive.

The woman who'd answered his knock was middle-aged and homely. When he'd gotten directions to Deputy Marts's home, he had more or less expected to find the man there with a wife. This woman had to be his mother. Or else young Horace Marts had a yen for women twice his age or thereabouts.

"I'm looking for Horace, ma'am."

She sniffed so primly and properly that Longarm thought Mrs. Marts should join the gang of biddies who were standing guard over Janet. She could fit right in with that crowd. "What would you be wanting of him?"

"I need your son's advice, ma'am. In his capacity as a lawman, that is."

The answer seemed to please the woman. For a moment there she looked almost pleasant. Almost. "Horace is out back mending some harness. That is where you will find him most evenings, I daresay."

"Yes, ma'am. Thank you."

There was a lean-to shed behind the Marts home. Longarm found the shed, but no sign of Horace. A box of tools and another of scraps were set out onto the tailgate of a decrepit excuse for a farm wagon, and a dry and dusty tangle of harness leather was collected in the box of the old wagon, but if anyone had worked on this mess any time in the past half-dozen years or so, Longarm would have been mighty surprised. Horace was out here working most evenings of late? Longarm didn't think so.

"Horace? You out here, Horace?"

There was no answer. Exactly. But after a moment Longarm heard a series of small sounds coming from behind the shed. "Horace?"

"Who are you? What do you want?" The sounds grew louder, and then Horace appeared, peeping out from a tangle of weeds that grew head tall against the side and back of the equipment shed. "Oh. It's you."

"I need t' talk to you, Horace. I need your help."

"Mine? You need *my* help?"

"Ayuh, I do."

"What can I do to help a federal marshal?" Marts asked.

"I need a couple warrants served, Horace. I been sorta

preoccupied in my room lately." Longarm grinned and winked.

"Yeah, I heard you had a little something there." Longarm wasn't surprised that Lee Xua's presence had been noticed by the townspeople, especially after the little confrontation he'd had with the waiter at breakfast. Normally he would resent gossip about his private affairs. This evening he was counting on it.

"Then you do understand. Good."

Marts squinted and cocked his head. There was the hot, slightly sour odor of cheap whiskey hanging in the air around him. "What are you paying?" he asked, suddenly suspicious.

"Dollar a paper," Longarm told him.

"They pay you two dollars for service," Marts responded.

"All right. A dollar and a quarter."

"Dollar and a half," the Fairplay deputy countered.

"Deal," Longarm said, sticking a hand out to shake. "How 'bout a drink to seal the bargain?"

"You buying?" Marts wanted to know.

"I'm buying. But listen, I don't want anybody t' know that I'm laying work off on you. This is strictly between the two of us, right?"

"I can keep a secret."

Longarm damn sure hoped not. But he wasn't going to come out and say so. Not to the man's face, he wasn't. "Tell you what," he said with a nod and a wink, "I'll go get us a bottle to share. Will anybody bother us if I bring it back here?"

"I can promise no one will disturb us here."

"Then you wait here, Horace. I won't be long."

"L-L-Longarm, m' ol' fren, you my bes' fren, y'know that?" Horace gave his new best friend a sloppy grin. It was an improvement. At least he was no longer drooling on himself. Longarm smiled back at him and offered Marts another pull at the nearly empty bottle.

"Mother's milk," Marts slurred. "'S' God's truf. Rye

whissey 's mother's milk.'' He swallowed a slug, belched, and helped himself to another. ''Fine,'' he mumbled. ''Migh'y fine.''

''So it is,'' Longarm agreed, retrieving the bottle and wedging the cork into its neck. Horace looked a trifle put out by that. But Jeez, Longarm didn't want the fool to get so drunk he was no good. ''Do me a favor, old friend?''

''Any . . .'' Horace burped again. ''Anything you wan', Longie m' boy.'' He giggled.

''I'm kind of curious.'' Longarm leaned close to Horace's ear and looked around to emphasize the degree of trust and secrecy that was between them now. ''As one peace officer to another, if you see what I mean . . .''

''Man t' man,'' Marts whispered loudly. ''Peace ossifer to peace ossifer. You an' me, ol' buddy 'n pal.''

''Right,'' Longarm said. ''Now what I want you to do, old friend . . .''

Chapter 30

Longarm stood outside the jail, waiting just far enough to the side so that Rodney Dewell would not be able to see him from the front office window.

It was not that Longarm did not trust Horace Marts to do what he wanted. It was more that he wasn't sure the drunken younger deputy could negotiate the half-dozen blocks between the jail and Marts's home. Not, at least, without assistance.

It was safer, Longarm figured, to wait just outside for him even if that did run the risk of Dewell discovering what was afoot.

"I got it!" Marts crowed as he stumbled out onto the sidewalk.

Longarm winced, sure Dewell had overheard. If he had, however, the night marshal failed to pay attention to the daytime deputy because there was no investigation of the overloud comment.

"C'mere," Longarm said, taking Marts by the elbow and

steering him into the shadows beside the jail. "Now quick, kid, where is it?"

The local boy cackled and reached under his coat, triumphantly withdrawing a crumpled sheet of butcher paper and showing it off to his very best friend in the whole wide world. "Here. Just like I tol' you I could do, ain't it?"

Longarm patted Marts on the shoulder—hell, he deserved some sort of reward for accomplishing the mission Longarm had sent him on—and accepted the paper. He smoothed it out and squinted, trying to make out the lead-pencil scratchings barely legible on the brown paper. In the end Longarm had to go back up onto the sidewalk and stand in the spill of lamplight from the jail to read the note.

GIRL ALIVE AN WELL. GIVE US 40,000 SPECIE NO PAPER. GET MONEY READY QUICK WELL—Longarm took that to mean "we'll," although it was not spelled that way—SEND NOTE AGAIN TELL YOU WHEN, WHERE YOU DELIVER. NO TRICKS OR THE GIRL DIES. NO TRICKS.

Longarm frowned and read the note through again. He opened his mouth to ask Marts what Faire and Kramer intended to do—after all, the kidnappers were asking double Harry's reward offer—but realized the futility of that before speaking. Horace Marts would be doing well right now if he could remember his own name, and under the best of circumstances he would not know what Harry Faire was capable of paying. As for Harry's willingness, though, Longarm had no doubt whatsoever. The man was devoted to his wife and to their daughter; he would do anything within his mortal power to get Elaine back unharmed. Within his mortal power, Longarm thought, or beyond it if Harry could find a way to make a swap with the devil. The girl seemed to mean that much to him. And to Janet.

"D' I do good, fren?" Horace asked, listing slightly to starboard as he came out of the shadows in a stiff-legged, uncertain walk to join his buddy and pal on the sidewalk. "D' I do what you wan'ned?"

"You did just what I wanted," Longarm assured him. "Do me one more favor, my friend?"

131

"Anything, L-Lon-garm."

"Take this back inside now an' put it back wherever they had it."

"Sure, Lon-garm, anything you wan." Horace grinned happily and took the gang's note back, stuffing it beneath his coat once more. Then, with a broad, conspiratorial wink, Marts laid his finger aside his nose and stumbled away in the general direction of the jail.

Longarm waited patiently for Marts to return, but when he did he was draped over the shoulder of Rodney Dewell. The excitement of it all—or maybe the whiskey'd had something to do with it—seemed to have gotten the better of young Horace, for he was passed out completely.

Satisfied that Horace was in good hands, and not especially anxious to confront Horace's mother when that formidable female discovered what her baby boy'd been up to this night, Longarm hung back out of sight until Horace and Rodney were well on their way to the Marts residence.

Then Longarm stepped out onto the street and strode away.

There were a couple more things he needed to do, a few more people he needed to see.

Then, by golly, he could amble on back to the hotel. And to little Lee Xua. He was looking forward to whatever the girl might come up with as an encore after her extraordinary early performances.

Chapter 31

It cost Longarm two dollars and fifty cents in liquor—he could have bought cheaper stuff but, hell, he had to drink it too—to get a look at the ransom note sent in by the kidnappers. It cost him two cents to find out how the note was delivered.

When he came down to breakfast in the morning there was another extra edition of the newspaper piled on the counter in the lobby. He contributed his two pennies, and carried a copy into the dining room with him.

This morning there was none of the previous day's bullshit about serving a Chinese in the same room where white folks were eating. The same waiter as yesterday came over just as politely as anyone could please and took their order. Not that there was all that much they needed. Longarm's stomach was a mite queasy after the rye he'd consumed while cajoling Deputy Marts into lending a hand, and Lee Xua had an appetite like a hummingbird. Which seemed a particularly apt simile. When she took his balls into her mouth and commenced to hum . . . he got his mind off that subject. There were more pressing matters to tend to right now. Besides, after a couple of nights with the energetic young Chinese, Longarm was on the sore side and was feeling purely worn out. Why, it might take as long as several hours to recover his abilities.

While they waited for their meal, Longarm laid the single folded sheet of newsprint out flat on the table and read the latest account of the Faire family tragedy.

The note was not directly quoted, nor was there mention in the paper about the gang's demand that Harry double the ransom. What interested Longarm the most was to learn that the note had turned up on a table in the parlor of a "sporting establishment" run by "a certain local entrepreneur of the female persuasion."

When the waiter came by with Longarm's coffee and Lee Xua's oolong tea, Longarm said, "This here, uh, sporting house. You wouldn't happen to know which one they're talking about, would you?"

The waiter gave Longarm an odd look, followed by a glance in Lee Xua's direction. Longarm could come up with half a dozen guesses at things the fellow could be thinking, given the question coupled with the open knowledge that the girl was staying in Longarm's room. Still and all, though, that was nobody's business but Longarm's and the girl's, and he wasn't about to volunteer any explanations to a stranger.

The waiter thought it over for a few seconds before he answered, but he probably believed—correctly—that the amount of tip he could expect at this table was riding on the response he gave. "I heard it was one of Sophie Mayberry's girls that found it," the man told him.

"And where might a gentleman find Miss Mayberry's place of business?"

The waiter gave Longarm another puzzled look. But he also gave directions to the whorehouse.

Sophie Mayberry's house of happiness might have been alluring as all hell at night, Longarm thought, but in the

134

harsh glare of morning sunlight it looked rundown and seedy. But then, day or night, the appeal of such a place wasn't so much the architecture or the lovely surroundings but something more on the practical side.

Longarm knew there was little likelihood he would find anyone in the working parlor at this time of day. The women who worked here should all still be sleeping after a hard night's labors, so he went around to the back door. If he'd thought the front looked rundown, he hadn't known the half of it; the back was a mass of litter and trash. He tried his luck at knocking there. A tall, angular black woman answered his rapping almost immediately, a finger at her lips to shush him. "You be quiet please, mister. You don't want to waken Miss Sophie or you won't walk out of here the same as you came. You'll leave things behind that no man ever wants to be without. If you take my meaning." She softened the warning with a smile, though.

"Actually, miss," Longarm said, taking out his wallet and opening it to display his badge, "I won't need to talk to Miss Mayberry if only you would let me speak with the young lady who found that note last night." He knew there was no need to specify the note he meant. Likely the talk in the parlor all night long had centered around that excitement.

"That would be Miss Daisy."

"Would it be too much trouble to wake her, please, and tell her she has a guest."

"A guest, is it? Well, at least you're being polite about it. Most coppers I know wouldn't bother."

"And Miss Daisy?" he asked.

"Set at the table there. I'll pour you some of that nice fresh coffee from off the stove and go fetch the young lady."

Longarm took his hat off and sat at the place indicated. The woman—he assumed she would be a cook and/or housekeeper—gave him the promised coffee and then whisked out of sight.

Chapter 32

Daisy came into the kitchen rubbing the sleep out of her eyes, yawning and stumbling and still only about half awake. At a guess Longarm would have said she was about the same age as Lee Xua and about the same height. But that was where the similarities ended.

Where Lee Xua was slender and vibrant, Daisy was plump and doughy, with rolls of fat only partially hidden under skin that had the pale, unhealthy hue of an unbaked pastry. She smelled of stale sweat and aging remnants of cheap perfume, and her breath when she said hello was foul and sour.

Streaks of dirt and last week's makeup collected in the folds of her skin like so many scars, giving her an almost grotesque appearance. Her hair was short and greasy and hung in ropy strands. Longarm had trouble trying to imagine why anyone would pay good money in order to bed a woman this repulsive. Of course, it was true that candlelight and whiskey could perform miracles. As Longarm could attest from personal experience. But *that* big a transformation? Surely even cheap Injun whiskey couldn't turn a sow like this one into silk.

Still, he was here not to judge the girl but to talk with her. He smiled and gave her a small bow, and held the chair for her to sit before joining her at the table. "You know who I am," he said.

"Bertie said you was a copper. Is that right?"

"Uh-huh. Deputy United States marshal."

"That's pretty good, in' it. I mean like, it's a big deal."

"Yeah, I think you could say that."

"Am I in trouble or anything?"

"Not at all," Longarm assured her. "I just want to ask you a few questions."

"About that paper I found, right? The one they say those bank robbers wrote? About the girl?" She shuddered and made a face. "I seen that girl at the bank sometimes. She's pretty. I hope they get her back all right."

"I hope so too, Daisy. And you can help make it happen." The girl brightened at that prospect and sat up straighter. Longarm said, "I want you to tell me the same things you told Marshal Kramer. That's all I need you to do."

The girl frowned and blinked. "Marshal Ed? I di'nt tell him nothing about the paper."

"You didn't?"

"Gosh, I ain't spoke to Marshal Ed in . . . I dunno . . . a couple weeks? He don't use none of the girls, see. I mean, he comes in all the time. But he never messes with none of us." She chuckled. "Miss Sophie would chop his balls off and slice an' fry them for mountain oysters if Marshal Ed went off with any of us working girls. He's private property, he is."

"I see, Daisy, but it isn't gossip I came here for, honey, it's information about that note you found."

"Sure, I don't mind telling you whatever, just so long as I ain't in trouble."

"No, hon, you're not in any trouble. In fact you can be a big help."

"I'd be glad to help you any way I can, Marshal."

"Good. Now just tell me the same things you told to whoever Marshal Ed had you talk to last night."

Again she frowned. "But I told you, I never talked with none of them."

"Pardon me? You haven't talked with any of them? Not even when you gave the note to them?"

"Oh, I never gave none of them that paper. I found it, like, on a side table in the parlor out there. I seen it an' thought somebody must of left it by accident, like, an' so I took it to Miss Sophie and asked her what it was an' if it was something important."

"You didn't know that from what it said?"

"What'd it say, Marshal?"

"You didn't read it when you picked it up?"

Daisy blushed. Longarm would not have thought her capable of it, but damned if the young woman didn't flush a bright rose that lent some life to her features and gave him a glimpse of what she might have looked like if she had chosen a more ordinary way of life for herself.

"You can't read, can you?" he asked.

She shook her head, her eyes down. "I never quite got the hang of them letters and stuff. I went to school, though. I did. And I can do pretty good with arithmetic. But reading and writing and spelling and all that stuff, none of it ever made much sense to me, like all them squiggles was just so many worms crawling around on the paper."

"It isn't anything you need to be ashamed of," Longarm said. "But . . . no one came to talk to you last night? About the note or who all was in and out of the parlor or any of that? Nobody?" Longarm found that to be downright incredible. After all, he did not like or trust Ed Kramer. But the man knew the correct procedures to follow. He might be a son of a bitch, but he knew how to handle an investigation. So why in the world would Kramer have failed to interrogate Daisy?

"Nobody," Daisy insisted, "but Miss Sophie woulda taken care of all that. After I found the paper an' gave it to her, she tol' me how important it was an' gave me a big kiss an' went rushing off someplace with it. I guess she woulda took it to Marshal Ed then, an' she woulda told the marshal an' his coppers anything they wanted to know."

Longarm grunted. That could make some sense, he supposed. Especially if Kramer and his people knew that Daisy could not read.

Surely, though, not only Daisy and Sophie but every man or woman who'd been inside the whorehouse last night should have been interviewed. After all, the ransom note hadn't blown in through a window on a whim of fate. It had been carried in by someone, presumably by one of the kidnappers, and left on that table where Daisy found it.

Surely Kramer would have—should have—tried to narrow the field of suspects by finding out exactly who'd visited the establishment last night.

"Would you do something for me, Daisy?"

"Sure, Marshal. Anything you want. Miss Sophie, she's all the time telling us to keep our noses clean an' always cooperate with the cops. Any of Marshal Ed's boys want anything, free trips to the rooms, anything at all, we're to do whatever they want. I know she'll want me to help out any way I can."

"That's nice, Daisy. What I want you to do, please, is to make out a list. I don't mean you have to write it down, mind; you can tell it to somebody and have them mark it down for you. Tell me everyone you can remember who was here last night. Everybody, mind. Not just the men, although I want to know who they were too, but also all the girls and any of the help working here, every human soul you can think of who walked into that room last night. Will you do that for me?"

"Sure, Marshal, I'll—"

The rest of her words were lost when the door leading into the kitchen slammed open with a crash.

"Out. Get out of here, you son of a bitch."

Longarm looked up, startled at this sudden appearance by an auburn-haired beauty who at the moment looked thoroughly pissed off.

The woman was probably in her early thirties. She had

a fine buxom figure with a narrow waist and a most shapely ass. Her hair hung loose and was uncombed—she'd almost surely been asleep until just moments ago—but gleamed with good health and frequent grooming. Her skin, cleansed of any makeup she might ordinarily employ, was smooth and fine, without blemish or blotch to mar her appearance. Had Longarm encountered her on a public street without knowing who she was, he would surely have taken her to be one of the community's leading matrons. And a damned fine-looking one at that. Under the circumstances . . .

He stood and bowed. "Miss Sophie Mayberry, I presume?"

"Unless you have a warrant to serve on me, you bastard, I want you out of my place. And right now, or I'll call Ed and have him arrest you on charges of trespass. Am I making myself clear?"

Longarm gave her a smile that he did not especially feel and said, "Can I finish my coffee first?"

"Out, damn you. Right now."

Longarm retrieved his Stetson and put it on. He gave Daisy a wink and looked past Sophie's shoulder to thank the very startled and upset cook, who probably was at least indirectly responsible for her boss's tirade. Likely, Longarm thought, the cook had informed Sophie of the visit as a matter of course. And now this.

What the hell. Daisy had said something about Kramer and Sophie being bedmates. He supposed it only natural that the woman would adopt her gentleman friend's prejudices along with everything else. Longarm bowed once more to Sophie and made a mildly hasty exit, lest the damned female make good on her threat and give Ed Kramer the extreme pleasure of being able to file legal charges against Longarm.

Chapter 33

Longarm took a pull on his cheroot and laid it carefully aside, fussily aligning the slim cylinder of dark tobacco leaf with the advertising slogan embossed on the bottom of the tin ashtray. He did it unconsciously, his thoughts directed intently on more important matters: Should he stay for one more card and hope to fill out a flush when the gent to his right had a pair of sevens showing and probably a matching third card in the hole . . . or should Longarm toss these in and wait for the next deal?

Normally he would not think twice about going for the flush. But sometimes a man has the feeling that things aren't going his way. With a snort that was half disgust with his own timidity and half annoyance that he was even bothering to think about such things, Longarm swept his cards together, turned them all facedown, and tossed them to the dealer. "Fold," he said, and left the table to get another drink.

When he came back he felt like kicking himself. The

141

town baker, a man named Eberday, had stayed on the strength of a pair of tens. And won the pot. The man with the sevens had nothing in the hole but bluster, and that hadn't been near enough. Longarm could have . . .

Could have. Never mind a bunch of could-haves. Longarm resumed his seat and picked up his cheroot, tapping the ash off and puffing to bring the coal back to life. Could have. Would have. Should have. Piss on a bunch of could-haves.

He was, he admitted, in a fairly shitty humor. He'd spent most of the afternoon sitting in Janet Faire's sickroom in the company of a succession of gray-haired old biddies all of them waiting for Janet to wake up from the doses of laudanum the local sawbones kept shoving down her throat.

The thing that was vexing Longarm the most was that those old women kept telling him that every time Janet came around she made the same damn request. She kept asking that Custis be brought to her. She kept insisting that there was something she had to tell him. No, no one else could deliver the message to him. She had to tell him herself.

Well, he'd been there, dammit. For hours. And all he saw was Janet sleeping. Janet barely breathing. Janet dying. It was . . . lousy. He hated it. And there was not one stinking thing he could do about it. He could only sit and watch her chest rise and fall with shallow, spasmodic effort. And worry.

God, he wanted to see the girl returned to her while there was yet time for Janet to comprehend the miracle of her child's safety. That was all Harry or Kramer or Longarm or anyone might still be capable of giving her. That and perhaps a slight lessening of the pain that ripped her gut and made her cry out even from within the depths of drugged unconsciousness. In truth Longarm did not blame the doctor for putting Janet under, even though she'd asked that she not be drugged. Bad as it was with the laudanum, it would have been ten times worse without the opiate.

Knowing all of that, though, did nothing to make Longarm feel any better about the situation, and earlier in the evening when Harry came home from his bank, he'd ordered Longarm out of the house.

"She's been asking for me, Harry. Surely it won't hurt nothing if I just continue t' set here quiet like I been."

"If she has anything to say I will send someone to find you. In the meantime, Custis, I will thank you to leave my house."

Longarm had had no choice but to comply. Like it or not, Harry had the right. It was indeed his damn house. "I'll be at the hotel," he'd said. That had been, what, five hours ago? Six? Surely Janet would have wakened by now. Surely she . . . he tried to make himself quit thinking about it. "I'm out," Longarm told the other players. "Cash me in."

He was down three or four dollars and didn't much give a shit. His attention hadn't been properly focused to begin with, and neither time nor whiskey was apt to change that for the time being. He stood, crushing the stub of cheroot out in the ashtray, and pocketed the coins he'd been playing with. "G'night, gentlemen."

"Any time, Long. Always glad to accept contributions."

Longarm left the rest of his drink on the table and went out into the lobby. He was sure there was no need, but he stopped at the desk and asked anyway.

"No, sir. Sorry but there haven't been any messages for you."

"If anyone is looking," Longarm said, "I'll be in my room."

"Yes, sir, of course."

He took the stairs slowly, feeling tired now and definitely out of sorts. If there was only something productive he could do, anything at all . . .

He tapped lightly on the door, and was pleased to hear Lee Xua draw the bolt before she could let him in. When he'd come up to get her for supper earlier, the room had been unlocked. He did not like that. Girls, especially girls whose skin was not snowy white, were always vulnerable. He did not want any harm to come to Lee Xua.

Longarm had to bend low to accept the girl's welcoming

143

kiss. She kissed him and gave him a fiercely happy hug, and began helping him out of his clothes.

Which he did not, in fact, mind even a little bit. There was something about this girl and the naturalness with which she waited on him that made him accept from Lee Xua personal attentions that would have embarrassed or rankled him if another woman were to make the same offer.

Once he was naked, Lee Xua tugged him into place—it didn't make any special sense to him, but she was downright intense about putting him into exact alignment with whatever impulse it was that drove her, more or less on the same order as him placing his cheroot just so in the ashtray downstairs—and had him stand there while she wet a cloth and soaked it and then began meticulously to bathe him. She soaped him, scrubbed him, carefully rinsed away every hint of soap, and then playfully commenced to lick his freshly washed nipples.

"You sure you wanta get this started?" he asked.

She tossed her head back and gave him an impish look. "I can finish whatever you start."

"Cocky, ain't you."

She looked down at his pecker, which was also so clean he expected it would squeak whenever it was rubbed. "Cocky, so."

"That wasn't exactly the sort o' cock I had in mind. But I reckon I could be convinced."

Lee Xua laughed—the reaction was probably her own sense of joy with life in general rather than anything he'd said, but he did not mind that—and dropped to her knees.

"You do that mighty well," he said. Lee Xua did not respond to the compliment. Well, not vocally anyway. She couldn't talk at that moment. Not with her mouth full.

"Wouldn't you be more comfortable on the bed?"

The girl nodded, but took her time about releasing him so he could go lie down.

Longarm laced his hands behind his head and plumped a feather pillow behind his neck. He wanted a good view of this performance. It was funny, but the more he was with this girl the better he liked her. And the longer he knew her, the more she allowed her playfulness to show.

While Longarm waited, she first blew a kiss in his direction, then picked up his brown Stetson and plopped it onto her own pretty head.

The hat was way the hell too large for her and came down onto the bridge of her nose, covering her ears and her eyes and making both of them laugh. Undaunted, Lee Xua swept her hair into an untidy pile and shoved that onto the top of her head. She put the hat over that, adding some stuffing that at least kept the Stetson from falling over her ears. Then she tilted the wide-brimmed hat back a little and laughed again. She looked cute as hell that way, Longarm thought.

"What I bring you?" she asked.

"You," he told her. "Just you."

Lee Xua grinned. "Good. One second, please. I turn light down. Make all cozy, okay?"

Longarm frowned. "Aw, I want to look at you while you do me."

"You look, okay, but turn light down. Too bright. Hurt my eyes, yes?"

He shrugged and Lee Xua, still wearing his Stetson, went to the small table beside the window. She leaned down to the lamp that was burning there.

And cried out as the sound of shattering glass filled the room.

The lightweight curtain over the window billowed inward, and the lamp was abruptly extinguished.

Half a heartbeat later Longarm heard the sickening crack of a muzzle blast, and a sense of dread washed through him like a flash flood of ice water.

Chapter 34

Lee Xua looked even smaller in death than she had in life. Tiny as she was, her body had held an amazing amount of blood, most of which was on the floor now. The bullet had taken her high in the chest, entering just left of center on her breastbone and angling slightly upward to exit between her shoulder blades. She would have died virtually instantaneously, Longarm saw. Which was a blessing of a sort, he supposed. At least the Chinese girl was not required to suffer the same agonies as Janet Faire for day after day before she died.

The angle of the wound indicated the shooter had stood at street level, probably in an alley across from the hotel between a cafe and a haberdashery. The rifleman was long gone now, of course. He'd taken his carefully aimed shot and then faded quickly into the shadows. All that was plain enough right on the surface of things.

But *why*, dammit? That was the question that kept gnawing at Longarm's gut.

Not why Lee Xua had died, that is. Hell, he understood that readily enough. When she'd leaned down to blow that lamp out, she must have thrown a shadow onto the thin cloth of the curtain at the front window. And since she'd been playfully wearing Longarm's Stetson, the assassin lurking somewhere outside mistook her figure for his, the difference in their sizes being lost because the shadow was projected onto the curtain at something greater than actual life size. So it was understandable—lousy but understandable—that a bullet intended for Longarm instead took the life of an innocent girl.

But why the fuck were the kidnappers so intent on getting rid of Longarm? Why their obvious fear of him? He didn't know anything that was a threat to them. He was sure of that. He hadn't yet figured out shit with this deal. So why had they made two attempts on his life: that first clumsy try by the rummy with a shotgun, and now this much better executed attack?

It wasn't making any sense to him.

But it was to somebody. Longarm knew he could count on that. The mere fact that he did not understand it did not alter the fact that it made perfect sense to *somebody*. Indeed it must surely be imperative for them to risk it. No one commits murder without a reason. That reason may not be a good one. But good or bad, well thought out or impulsive rage, there was, there must be, a reason.

It was just that Longarm failed to comprehend what the reason could be here.

Dammit, he'd gone to great lengths to demonstrate that he was not involved in the robbery and kidnap case, that this investigation belonged solely to the local marshal.

They'd tried to kill him anyway. Why?

"Why?" Rodney Dewell asked.

Longarm blinked, forcing himself to pay attention to the present time and place. He could do his speculating later.

"Seems an awful waste, doesn't it?" the Fairplay night marshal observed, looking down at the dead girl.

Lee Xua was naked, of course. Longarm knew that made no difference really. And hell, she'd been a whore for the kin who'd brought her into the country. But that hadn't altered the fact that Longarm had taken a genuine liking to the girl. She'd been sweet and giving and full of zest, and she damn sure hadn't deserved to end up naked on a grimy hotel room floor with strangers staring at her tits. Longarm pulled a blanket off the foot of the bed he and Lee Xua so recently shared, and used it to cover her. If the hotel wanted to be as nasty about her blood staining their blanket as they'd been about her presence in their precious whites-only dining room, then the hell with them.

"Did she have any enemies, Long?"

"Not that I know of. She had a disagreement with her cousins, who seemed t' think they owned her for a slave. But killing her wouldn't make much sense, not when they were wanting her back to work for them again it wouldn't."

"Anyone or anything else?"

Longarm shook his head. He was not particularly inclined to explain to Dewell that the slug that killed Lee Xua was surely intended for him and not her. That would just bring Ed Kramer and the rest of the local law into the picture, and right now Longarm did not really want them or anybody else messing into his personal, private business.

And this deal was damn sure personal to him now. It had been before really, with Janet lying there dying while her daughter was in the hands of kidnappers. But now, with an innocent girl dead, and one who'd been under Longarm's protection at that, it had gotten doubly so. He took this case of mistaken identity very personally indeed.

"D'you need me for anything more, Rodney?"

The night marshal shook his head.

"Then I'm gonna move my things into another room and get out of your way. You'll take care o' the body?"

"Yeah, I expect I'll have to. You don't know where I can find those cousins of hers, do you?"

"No, I don't. They're both named Lee something-or-other. I forget exactly what. I assumed they were living here in town, but I never actually asked."

"We'll ask around, see if we can find some kin to claim the body. These Celestials, they like to be pickled in brine

148

and packed into barrels and shipped back to wherever they came from in China for burying. Did you know that?''

Longarm had, but he didn't want to ruin Dewell's display of exotic information by saying so.

''If we can't find her people I expect we'll put her under as a pauper,'' Dewell added.

''If you can't find her cousins, Rodney, let me know. She was a nice girl. Deserves better than Potter's Field. If it comes to that I'll pay for the burial.''

''That's damned decent of you, Long. I didn't think . . . uh, never mind.''

Longarm gathered up his things and went to arrange for a change of hotel room. Apart from the mess in this one, he did not want somebody out there on the street making another try for him with a rifle. Next time there would not be some innocent there to take the bullet in Longarm's place.

But Lee Xua. Little, sweet, pretty Lee Xua. Damn it all to hell and back anyway.

Chapter 35

There was a lamp burning in Harry Faire's study. Longarm glanced around to make sure he was not observed, then slipped over the picket fence that surrounded the Faire place and made his way through the shadows to the carefully tended flower bed outside the study. A quick look inside showed him that Harry was alone. Longarm went around to the back of the house and let himself into the kitchen without knocking.

He could hear someone talking in the upstairs hallway, no doubt part of the contingent of faithful biddies who watched over Janet day and night. Longarm ignored them and went into the foyer and through it to the study.

"Custis. You startled me." Faire got up from the wing-back chair where he'd been busy reading through a thick sheaf of papers. He extended a hand and warmly shook.

"How is she tonight, Harry?"

"No improvement. But no worse either. The doctor insisted on giving her more laudanum. The dosage is becoming dangerously heavy in order to keep her in some degree of comfort, but"—Harry shrugged—"what are the choices. I can't bear to stand idly by and allow her to suffer. And the doctor tells me it is for the best."

"When you get Elaine home"—Longarm was very careful to avoid using the word "if"—"when your girl comes home you have to let Janet come out of the drug long enough that she knows."

Harry nodded unhappily. Not that there was anything of late that he could pretend to be happy about anyway. Life had not been treating him very kindly. "Why are you here tonight, Custis? I thought you told me last night that you wouldn't risk coming again until we heard again from Elaine's kidnappers."

Longarm explained briefly about Lee Xua's murder. "I can't figure this out, Harry. Why are they trying to kill me? You haven't slipped up and mentioned to anybody, have you, that you and me aren't really on the outs?"

"Of course not. We agreed to this when we talked in my office, and I haven't said a word to anyone except what you said you wanted. The reward to make sure the gang had good reason to keep Elaine alive, and a make-believe conflict between the two of us so none of them would know they were the subject of two separate investigations, Ed's and yours too."

"Damn," Longarm complained. "I was almost hoping you'd let the cat out of the bag. At least then I could understand why they'd feel that my presence was a threat to them."

"Could these attempts on your life be unrelated to the robbery and kidnapping, Custis? Could this be the work of some disgruntled felon you arrested some time in the past?"

"I thought about that o' course, Harry, but I can't think of anybody likely. Haven't seen or heard about anyone bein' up here who might have a grudge against me. Besides, I can't much believe in coincidence like that. No, old friend, I pretty much gotta believe that whatever reason these fellas have for wanting me out of the way, it's something to do with your girl and the door to Hell those boys opened when they took her. They're scared o' me. They must be. But I'm damned if I know why." Longarm sighed.

"You look tired. Can I offer you a drink?"

"I'd like that, Harry. Thanks."

While Harry fixed drinks for both of them, Longarm slumped into one of the exceptionally comfortable chairs that furnished the study. "I don't suppose Janet has been awake enough to tell you what message it is that she's trying to get t' me?" he asked, head back against the upholstery and eyes closed. Lordy, he was tired. First Janet and the girl. Now Lee Xua. It was too much. Just too damned much for a man to take. He wanted to fight back. If only he knew who he needed to fight.

"She came around a little this evening before the doctor got here and put her back under. I asked her. I promised you last night that I would, and I did ask her, Custis. She told me it was something she had to discuss with you alone. God only knows what it could be. We've never had any secrets between us. Not even about . . . you know . . . how it was with you and her back when we were kids."

Longarm nodded. "I'm glad for that, Harry. It shows what a good marriage you two have had. You want t' know something? I kinda envy you the way it's been for the both of you. Not that I coulda given her anything like the fine life you have. An' it ain't money that I'm talking about here. You've been a better husband to Janet than I ever could have. Hell, she knows that too. She told me so when we had coffee the other morning, before she came to work an' got caught in the middle o' that robbery." Harry handed Longarm a glass of rye, and Longarm downed half of it in one long gulp. "Jesus, Harry, I wish I'd kept her talking there a spell longer."

"Don't we both, Custis. Don't we both."

Chapter 36

Longarm jumped at the sound of a knock on his door. Two days he'd been waiting at the hotel, most of that time locked inside his room with an unread book and a sour disposition. Harry had promised to get word to him when either of two things happened: when Janet regained her senses or when the second ransom note was delivered. This knock surely had to be one or the other.

"Coming." He was eager for the news but not stupid. Or anyway, he hoped not, especially with someone in Fairplay gunning for him. He had no reason to believe that his adversary, whoever it was and whatever his reasons, would decide to quit after two failed attempts. He picked up his Colt and took it with him to the door, standing well to the side before he spoke again. Just in case. "Who is it?"

"It's me, Marshal. Rodney Dewell."

Longarm frowned. And opened the door. "Come in, Rodney."

The night marshal was not Harry's messenger, that was

for sure. Longarm motioned him into the room's only chair and returned the .44 to its holster. "I have some rye whiskey here, Rod. Would you care for a jolt?"

"No, thanks, I'm working."

"A smoke then? These cheroots are mighty good."

"No, but I thank you for the offer."

Longarm got a cheroot and matches off the bedside table and began trimming the twist, then struck the match and first let the sulfur burn off before he ran the flame beneath the barrel of the cigar to warm the tobacco before he lighted it.

"The reason I stopped by," Dewell said, "is I thought you'd want to know that we located the Chinese girl's folks. They're over in Leadville. They sent word they'll be along in a few days to claim the body and send it home. Wherever that is."

Longarm nodded. He did not show it, but in truth he was relieved. Being buried among one's ancestors was important to the Chinese, or so he understood. Lee Xua likely would have been grateful, glad to know she would be going home instead of spending eternity in the company of strangers. Dewell's news was a pathetically small victory. But at least it was a victory of sorts, which any form of good news would be after all the unrelenting troubles these past days. "Thanks, Rod. It's nice o' you to go to this trouble."

"Yes, sir. Well, um, that isn't the only reason I dropped in to see you this evening."

"Oh?" Longarm puffed on his smoke and let a series of puffy rings form in front of his lips to begin floating toward the ceiling, twisting and deforming as they rose. "What other good news d'you have for me?"

"No other good news actually. But, well, I thought you ought to know." Dewell was not looking at Longarm now. He had his hands locked in his lap and was paying close attention to his own tightly laced fingers.

"Trouble, Rodney?"

"I hope not. I mean, that's why I came here, sort of. To keep there from being any trouble." He twisted his fingers some more, his concentration still focused on them. "I mean, well, I've heard the marshal talk about you, Longarm. But you seem square to me, and I don't . . . I mean, well . . ."

"What's fixing to happen, Rod?"

"Tomorrow, well, the marshal said tomorrow he's going to make you leave Fairplay."

"Is that a fact?" Longarm formed one more perfect smoke ring and sent it drifting toward the window.

"He said he's going to file charges against you for trespassing on private property, and he's going to wire a formal protest to your boss down in Denver and then have the local magistrate order you taken into custody. If you don't accept the irons willingly, then he'll deputize a bunch of fellows and make you take it like it or not."

"I see." Longarm puffed on his cheroot for a few seconds while he gave the news some thought. Then he smiled just a little. "Ed knows you're here, doesn't he, Rod?"

Dewell looked thoroughly miserable. He wrung his hands and still would not look Longarm in the eye. "He . . . I guess I might have mentioned to him that you seem like a right enough fella to me. So tonight he told me to come up here and warn you about tomorrow."

"Uh-huh. And I take it I'm supposed to avoid a confrontation by taking the morning train down to Denver?"

"I . . . he never said anything about that. Exactly."

"But that's what you would take it to mean? The reason why he wanted you to tip me to the plan for tomorrow?"

"I'd say prob'ly so, yes."

"All right, Rod. Thank you for telling me."

"Can I ask you something?"

"Sure."

"Are you . . . I mean . . . what will you do tomorrow?"

Longarm smiled at him. "It might be you're better off not knowing that. After all, I wouldn't want t' put you in a position of havin' to take sides between me and your boss. That wouldn't hardly be fair."

Dewell looked half grateful for that bit of consideration and half upset not to be let in on Longarm's intentions. He thought for a moment, then looked up at Longarm and smiled back. "You aren't going, are you? You won't let the marshal buffalo you."

"Now that isn't exactly what I said, Rod. Was it?"

Fairplay's nighttime lawman looked at Longarm and grinned. "No, sir. You didn't say that. Quite."

"Thank you for telling me, Rod. Both things."

"Yes, sir." Dewell stood and remained there for a moment, uncertain if he should say anything more. In the end he decided against it and settled for sticking his hand out to shake. "It's been a pleasure, sir. Oh, and if it makes any difference . . . if things come to a head tomorrow I won't be coming along with the rest of the fellows. I expect I'll be sound asleep when that time comes."

"I appreciate that, Rod. G'night now."

"Good night, sir." Dewell let himself out, and Longarm bolted the door shut behind him.

Chapter 37

"There's someone to see you. Outside." The waiter sounded so pleased with the news that Longarm didn't have to wonder who it was. It would be Kramer. And ten to one the waiter would sneak out to have a look, hoping to see Longarm humiliated. Well, lots of luck, fella, Longarm thought.

"Aren't you going to—"

"When I finish my coffee," Longarm said.

"Can I tell him that?"

"Mister, I don't much give a shit what you wanta do."

The waiter smirked and turned away. Longarm guessed there must be quite a few of the locals waiting for him out there.

He sat where he was and slowly drank his coffee right down to the last drop. Then he left change on the table to pay for the meal plus a one-cent tip. Longarm hoped the asshole waiter accepted that in the spirit in which it was given.

He went out to the lobby, and again took his time looking over his bill and signing the slip they would present along with the voucher for the government to pay. "You have my things there?"

"Yes of course, Mr. Long. Right here." The clerk brought Longarm's carpetbag, saddle, and Winchester out from behind the counter. Longarm wedged the saddle and scabbard under his left arm and took up the carpetbag in his left hand as well. He wanted his right hand free. Just in case.

"Come again, sir," the clerk said, likely not meaning a word of it but saying it anyway. After all, in addition to Longarm's own questionable popularity among the hotel staff and certain of the local citizens, there was the small matter of a young woman dying, and rather messily at that, in his room. No, he seriously doubted that the personnel of this hotel looked forward to a repeat visit by this particular guest.

Longarm shoved his way through the double doors onto the sidewalk. Town Marshal Ed Kramer was there, all right. So were Horace Marts and two other deputies, plus some hangers-on who might have been with Kramer and his bunch, or who might simply have come along in the hope of having a ringside seat at a gunfight. Longarm often wondered about the sort of imbecile a man would have to be in order to volunteer to put himself in the line of fire from stray bullets. But any time there was a threat of deadly confrontation, there was always some fool who just had to run see it for himself.

"I think you know why I'm here, Long," Kramer announced in an unnaturally loud voice. "Are you going to tuck your tail between your legs and run, or do you want us to take you to jail in manacles?" Kramer lent some drama to the situation, or maybe was trying to bolster the spirits of his bullies, by holding up a pair of exceptionally heavy handcuffs, the old-fashioned kind with a solid steel bar through which miniature ox-yoke cuffs were affixed.

Longarm did not immediately respond. Instead he set his things down and slowly, deliberately took out a cheroot and lit it. He held the cigar at a jaunty angle between his teeth and looked past Kramer to Deputy Marts.

"Come for those warrants I asked you t' serve did you, Horace?"

The young deputy looked embarrassed. "I, uh, I won't be doing no piecework for you after all."

"Yeah, well, whatever," Longarm said past the end of his cheroot.

"What's that about? What now?" Kramer asked. Obviously Marts hadn't confessed anything to his boss about the wet evening he'd spent with Longarm. And he damn sure would not have admitted to sneaking the ransom note out for Longarm to read.

"What's your charge, Ed?"

"Trespass. You know that."

"At your girlfriend's whorehouse? C'mon now, Ed. How d'you figure to get a jury t' buy that trumped-up horseshit."

"I already got a magistrate to sign a warrant. Is that good enough for you?"

"Somehow, Ed, it don't much surprise me."

"So what will it be, Long? Are you going to resist the orders of a duly authorized peace officer in the performance of his duties?"

Longarm puffed on his cigar for a few moments. Then he looked Kramer in the eye. "Ed, I kinda hate t' do this. But I'm gonna ruin all your fun."

"How's that, Long?"

"I already sent a boy over to the livery this morning. They got a horse waiting for me there right now. I'm gonna take the easy way out an' get outa your town. I got work t' do, y'see. Official business for the government o' the United States. I reckon that's more important than seeing you back water."

Kramer looked shocked. His deputies looked relieved. The spectators looked damned well disappointed.

"You're welcome to come see me off," Longarm offered, bending down to pick up his things, this time taking the carpetbag in his right hand as a further proof there would be no trouble on the street this morning.

Ed Kramer scowled. But there was not a damn thing he could do at this point to lend fuel to the fire. There were too many witnesses present to let him manufacture any new excuse for a fight. He turned and angrily pointed a finger at one of his deputies, then jerked the thumb of the same hand toward the east end of town, where the livery stable was located. "You, Larry. Go with him. After you see him ride past the town limits, you come find me and tell me he really did turn tail and run rather than resist me."

Not that it was Ed Kramer who Longarm would have been resisting, but the entire weight of civil law. But then, Longarm thought, that was probably putting too fine a point on things for a man like Kramer to appreciate.

Without looking back—he didn't need to see the expression on that dining room waiter to know that he was leaving a mighty happy man in his wake—Longarm marched off toward the livery.

Chapter 38

Longarm waited until midnight or thereabouts before he sneaked back into town. He came in from the north, avoiding the main roads and walking the horse quietly through a residential neighborhood. He found the street he wanted, the next street over from the one the Faires lived on, and guided the horse through yards and past dark windows so that he came up on Harry's house from behind.

Even then he took nothing for granted, tying the horse in the yard of one of Harry's neighbors and reconnoitering on foot through the neighborhood to make sure none of Kramer's people—or any would-be assassins—had been posted outside in the event he did precisely what he was doing by coming back unannounced and at night. After all, it was not exactly unknown that Janet Faire wanted to tell him something. Someone other than himself and Harry could have figured out that Longarm would want to see Mrs. Faire again before he left Fairplay.

If there was anyone hiding in the bushes, though, he was

too good for Longarm to spot. And modesty aside, Longarm considered that possibility to be pretty damned improbable. Satisfied that no one was about, he once again let himself in through the back door and tiptoed on through to the study where, this time, Harry was expecting him.

There! Movement. He was sure of it although it was dark and the road was in deep shadows at this point.

The rider was alone, a single horseman followed closely by a burro that probably wasn't a third as big as the horse. The burro had an unnatural lump on its back. That would be the gold. But then $32,000 in specie weighs a helluva lot. You don't drop that kind of money into a saddlebag and wander away. Not hardly.

Horse and burro were moving slowly. The rider seemed in no hurry, and obviously knew right where he was going.

The deal was that Marshal Kramer was to deliver the gold. He was to ride alone and unarmed—at considerable risk to himself if so—to meet the kidnappers and exchange the gold for the girl.

The second ransom note, as the first one had, demanded that Harry double the offered reward to $40,000, but the man quite honestly had not been able to raise that much cash. Even by borrowing from his fellow bankers after cleaning out his own accounts, he hadn't been able to scrounge together more than the $32,000 that he'd now entrusted to Kramer.

Harry would have paid out more if he'd been able. Longarm was sure of that. The man would have done literally anything within his power in order to save his daughter's life and to give Janet one moment of peace before she died. But $32,000 was the absolute limit of what he could raise on short notice.

Kramer had advised him—and Longarm had later concurred—that the gang was unlikely to wait in the hope of getting more money, but that they would probably—there were no guarantees—settle for the lesser amount and let the girl go. It was the old cliché about the bird in hand being a helluva lot more valuable than future expectations. And it was true.

So now there Kramer went, alone in the night, to let himself be surrounded by a bunch of bank robbers, kidnappers, and would-be assassins.

The note said he was to ride out on the road to Hartsel and keep going until he was met by someone who would say "Thursday"—it wasn't—and he was to respond "cayuse." Kramer was to drop the burro's lead rope. The kidnappers would bring out the girl blindfolded and mounted on a slow horse. At that point each party was to go its own way.

The plan sounded fine. As long as everyone involved did exactly as they said they would. Which in Longarm's experience was a damned seldom sort of thing. Still, it was the deal that had been decided upon, and they were going with it.

With one wild card thrown into the deal unbeknownst to either the kidnappers or to Ed Kramer.

None of them had any inkling that Longarm was there keeping a fatherly eye on it all. And with any luck whatsoever, none of them would ever have to know.

He stood for another few moments on top of the ridge overlooking the road, then slipped down to the other side of the rise and stepped into his saddle, guiding the horse on a course parallel to the public road and just out of sight from it.

Chapter 39

They worked it slick as snot on ice. One minute it was just the horse and burro plodding along. The next the road was full of horses and riders. Well, at least it was a lot more full than it had been.

The riders had been waiting in some brush that flanked the meandering trout stream—Longarm thought this inconsequential little step-across creek was supposed to be the headwaters of the South Platte River, but wasn't positive about that—in country that looked like a jackrabbit couldn't hide in it, although in fact there were three horses and three riders very effectively hidden there, mostly by the simple but nearly always workable expedient of remaining motionless. Day or night, but especially at night, it was movement that caught the eye. And these boys handled themselves just fine, remaining still as stone until Kramer and the burro were past, then coming out onto the road smack dab behind him. If Kramer was as startled to find them breathing down his neck as Longarm was to suddenly see them, then it was a wonder the Fairplay marshal didn't shit his drawers.

Kramer came to a stop and for five, six minutes he and the kidnappers palavered. Longarm wished to hell he was close enough to hear what was being said, but that would have been stupid. It would have been one thing for him to up and risk Ed Kramer's life—wouldn't be any real loss if one of the gang shot him—but it would have put Elaine at risk too. And that Longarm would not do. He had to settle for watching from afar while Kramer handled the face-on meeting with the kidnappers.

After a while they must have reached some sort of accord, because one of the kidnappers took the lead rope to the burro and forded the creek with it. A few seconds later the other two gang members followed, while Kramer turned his horse around and set off back toward Fairplay.

The only thing wrong was that there hadn't been any exchange for the girl.

Where the hell was Elaine Faire and why was Kramer going back without her?

It could have something to do with the $8,000 shortfall from what the kidnappers demanded, he supposed. But why the hell was Kramer turning over the money without getting the girl? Surely the idiot hadn't actually come out here unarmed? Never mind that he was supposed to. Longarm sure as hell hadn't expected him to.

And now . . . Longarm scowled. Now there wasn't much for it except to trail along and see what came next, and the hell with Ed Kramer and his timidity.

The three kidnappers, now with the gold-laden burro in tow, cut across country until they reached an old road that led off to the east. They turned onto it and increased their speed, none of them with any idea that Longarm was jogging along behind and beside their line of travel.

Before too long he figured out that they were heading for Bailey. Or anyway, for what used to be called Bailey. It had been one of those short-lived boom towns, growing like a mushroom during the original Pikes Peak gold rush.

Or so Longarm had been told. He hadn't been around that long ago. He had been through what was left of the town in more recent years. Most of the old buildings had been constructed of aspen logs, and those did not last long. The houses and storefronts were mostly fallen down, those that hadn't been torn apart and burned as campfire wood in the years since Bailey and Tarryall and those other early placer mining camps were abandoned in favor of more durable diggings like Fairplay and Alma to the west.

Nowadays there probably wouldn't be half a dozen folks with reason to pass through Bailey in a year's time.

Which, he acknowledged, was plenty good enough reason for a gang of kidnappers to hole up there.

It surprised him some to discover this, though, because he thought he'd talked to enough people that their passage on any of the roads—or for that matter across the hills and open grasslands—to reach the area would surely have been noted. And reported back either to him personally or to one of the Fairplay officers. Four or five riders and a girl damn sure should have been noticed, but they'd gotten through somehow.

Well, it didn't matter now how they'd slipped through then. The point was, now Longarm had them in sight.

And he did not much expect to let them get away.

Chapter 40

Longarm made sure his Colt had all six chambers full and that the Winchester's pipe was stuffed to the brim as well, plus a round in the chamber. This could turn into one of those situations where firepower was more important than safety. Then he left the horse tied to a sapling, and made his way on foot toward what was left of a cabin hidden in the hills just west of the once-thriving ghost town.

It was coming dawn, and obviously the newly rich kidnappers did not intend to go back to sleep. Longarm could smell bacon and woodsmoke as he neared the cabin. It reminded him of how long it had been since supper last night, and made his mouth water. If they had some coffee to go with the bacon, he would have to help himself to some breakfast once the job at hand was tended to.

He came up behind the place and got a closer look at the setup. When he did he was pissed off. Thoroughly.

Two wagons were parked behind the cabin, and there

were four horses and the burro contained in a freshly rebuilt corral there. Two wagons.

Two fucking wagons that Longarm was sure he'd seen before.

He'd seen them, dammit, the same day of the robbery and kidnapping. With four young "farmers" heading— why, driving in this direction, come to think of it, coming from the direction of Trout Creek Pass and heading this way.

Longarm felt a surge of bitterness. The wagons had seemed empty at the time save for some tarps piled loosely behind the driving boxes. Elaine Faire must have been hidden under one of those tarps. Probably the gang's saddles had been under the other.

How in the hell could he have been so . . .

Easily. That was how they'd fooled him. In the easiest way possible. The sons of bitches had "hidden" in plain sight. Which was often the very best way to hide. Likely they had ridden pell-mell from town to wherever the wagons had been hidden, then switched from saddles to harness and quickly changed their own appearances as well—the "cowboys" who'd robbed the bank suddenly became "farmers" driving their wagons down a well-traveled public road in plain sight of God and everybody. And who would have thought that a slow-moving farm wagon was the gang's getaway vehicle. Nobody would be that dumb. Except these boys had been that clever, damn them.

And the worst part was that it had worked. They had flummoxed him completely.

Until now.

Longarm checked to see that his Colt was loose and free in the leather, then dragged the Winchester's hammer back to full cock.

Moving quiet as a morning fog, he slipped closer and closer to the cabin and to the kidnappers inside it.

"Goddammit, we got to kill her. We got the money. There ain't more to be had. Now we got to do what we got to do, else she'll put the law on us."

"She won't do that. Ask her."

"My God, Willy, you'd take her word for that? Hell, son, I can't believe even you would be that stupid. She'll promise you anything in order to save her own life. So would I. That don't mean she'll stick with her word once she's safe at home with her mama and her daddy. You know she'll tell. Anybody in their right mind would tell. Tell what we look like, what our names are, everything. It ain't like we've kept our mouths shut around her or covered her eyes or anything. She knows near about all there is to know about every damn one of us. Now the fact is, we got to kill her. Go ahead and fuck her first if you like. Have fun. But when everybody's had all the pussy he wants, boys, the girl has to go under. That's the way it is. It's her or us, and I damn sure ain't gonna let it be me that goes under instead of her."

Longarm knelt beneath the empty gap that served as a window in the side wall of the old cabin. If there had ever been glass in the window, which wasn't likely, it was long since broken and gone. He could hear clearly from this close up, and he was sure he'd heard those same voices before, which made him all the angrier to have been fooled.

"I won't let you do that to her, Al," the one called Willy said. "You'd have to get past me to reach her, and that won't be no piece of cake."

"You best be careful who you threaten, son, because it's no more bother to dig a hole for two than it is to make a hole for one. And your share of the money would go real nice split up amongst the rest of us. Three ways instead of four sounds all right to me. Think about that, Willy. Then you decide what's best, you hear?"

"But she's a really nice girl. She . . ."

"Willy," a new and gentler voice cut in.

"Yes, Leon?"

"I'm sorry, but Al is right. We can't let her go. It would be suicide, and the rest of us won't let you do that to us. But don't you worry. We won't ask you to kill her, and if it makes you feel any better, Willy, I'll promise she won't feel hardly a thing. I won't let her linger and hurt. All right?"

"You swear to God, Leon? You'll kill her quick?"

"Cross my heart, Willy."

"Thank you, Leon."

Jeez, these old boys were considerate, Longarm thought. Extort a fortune from the girl's father in exchange for her life, then kill her anyway. But mercifully. They should get full credit for that. They were only going to kill her, not make her suffer like her mother was.

Yeah, these old boys were the very salt of the earth, they were.

Helpful, though. Thanks to their conversation Longarm could be sure there weren't any more inside the cabin than the four he already knew about. Which would explain why three of them had gone to collect the ransom. Three to handle any fighting that was needed and the fourth staying back to watch the girl.

Sons of bitches.

Longarm slipped silently around to the front. There was only one door. And it was fixing to let the fires of Hell blow in on those ol' boys in there.

Chapter 41

The door was latched, but that was no problem. The thick wooden latch was only built to keep out blizzards and bears and minor annoyances like that. No way could it withstand the fury that burned in Longarm's belly.

He leveled the Winchester in his left hand and palmed the Colt in his right. Then, with a roar like that of a raging lion, he kicked the door open and burst in behind it.

One of the men had been standing just inside with a bucket in his hand. He might have been on his way out for water. Longarm did not stop to inquire. He pressed the muzzle of the Winchester against the startled kidnapper's chest and pulled the trigger. The force of the blast sent the man staggering backward, and the muzzle flash set his shirt on fire. By then, however, the fellow was incapable of feeling flame on flesh. He fell sprawling across a three-legged table, sending it and whatever had been on it into the lap of the man named Al.

Willy had been seated on one of the rope-sprung bunks

against the wall to Longarm's right. He came to his feet with a shout, and Longarm shot him, the hastily aimed slug flying high and smashing into Willy's forehead.

A man standing beside the stove with a spatula in one hand dropped the utensil and spun around to reach for a shotgun propped in a far corner. Longarm put a bullet between that one's shoulder blades—it was not a sporting target, but then gunfighting was not generally regarded as a sport, especially by those who were participating in it—and the man dropped, dead before his face hit the floor.

Al was the only one left, and he had a lap full of table, cornbread dough, and thanks to his dead partner, blood.

"Halt," Longarm said in a dry voice, "you are under arrest."

Then without waiting for an answer he shot Al in the face.

That too would have been considered unsporting. But what choice did he have. If he waited, damn it, the bastard might actually have surrendered.

Longarm checked the one in the corner—the others he was already sure of—but that one was dead too. Satisfied that there was no more opposition capable of shooting at him, he shoved the Colt into its holster and strode across the single room of the old cabin.

The girl was huddled beneath a blanket on the bunk in the back corner of the place. Even from a distance he could see that she was naked, with a filthy scrap of blanket pulled over her. She was trembling violently, probably scared half to death by the sudden noise and violence and blood.

"It's all right," Longarm said gently. "Let's find your things now an' take you home to your folks."

The girl's eyes were huge and she seemed speechless. But the word "home" got a response. Elaine squeezed her eyes tight shut and began to cry.

"It's all right now, honey," he assured her. "They won't none of them hurt you ever again. I promise."

He had to strain to hoist the bag of gold coins into the back of the wagon. He'd chosen the better of the two, and

172

hitched two of the kidnappers' horses to it, then tied the remaining horses and the burro to the tailgate.

He went inside and checked on the girl. She looked like she'd been through Hell. Well, she had at that. She was entitled to that vacant, hopeless look. Get her home, with a hot bath, some fresh-baked goodies in her stomach, and people she loved there to fuss over her, and she would soon enough get to both looking and feeling better. He wasn't overly worried about that.

Elaine was a pretty girl, he saw, in spite of her current bedraggled appearance. Pretty and somehow familiar to him, even though he was absolutely certain that he'd never laid eyes on her in his life.

And it wasn't that she looked like her mother either, because she didn't. For some reason, though, she looked awfully familiar to him. He couldn't figure out why.

"Here, put this blanket around your shoulders. It's kinda chilly this morning. You want more o' that bacon? There's a couple chunks left."

The girl shook her head, so Longarm helped himself to what was left of the bacon the one in the corner had been cooking. There was no coffee, though. The pot had gotten knocked over in all the excitement, so Longarm would have to wait until they got back to Fairplay before he could have his morning coffee.

"Ready?"

Elaine nodded silently, and Longarm took her elbow and walked her slowly out to the wagon, then helped her up into it. He went around to the other side and climbed up beside her, shaking the reins out and taking a light contact with the driving bits. "Hyup now, boys. Let's go." The wagon rolled forward with the sound of iron tires crunching gravel. The bodies he left behind. There would be time enough to send someone out to tend to them later on.

Longarm let the first few miles go by without speaking. Then he asked, "Mind if I smoke?"

Elaine shook her head, and Longarm went about the small tasks of firing up a cheroot.

"I can see how you wouldn't wanta talk to any strangers

173

right now," he said quietly, directing his words in the general direction of the near wheeler's butt, "but it might help if you'd listen for a minute. That all right with you?"

Still the girl did not speak, but he thought he saw her shoulders rise and fall in a very small shrug. He took that as a sign of approval and went ahead.

"What I want t' mention to you is that nobody alive on this earth, nobody except you, has any notion of what-all went on inside that cabin. You hear me?" He didn't wait for an answer, which was just as well, because she did not offer one.

"Anybody wants to think things or make assumptions, that's up to them. But the only things anybody will know for sure, girl, is what you tell them. Mind, though. What you tell to any one lone soul is apt t' be repeated. That's human nature. You can't change it. So you decide what you want folks around you to know, and then you say whatever you're willing for the whole world t' know along with those that you choose t' confide in."

She turned her head and gave him a look that he couldn't quite interpret. Damn, she did look familiar. But why? He couldn't figure that.

"As for me, there's nothing I can say to anybody about what happened back there. Oh, there's some will ask, o' course. But the only thing I know for certain sure, an' therefore the only thing I can say, is what I actually seen. An' that was just a few seconds o' shooting an' cussing. Nothing more. You hear me?"

She nodded, thought for a moment, and then nodded again, this time more firmly.

"Good," he said, drawing the tasty smoke deep into his lungs and exhaling it into the crisp air of a mountain morning. If those men had done anything to Elaine, well, he was in no position to make claims about it. He hadn't seen a damn thing that would compromise her. And no one would ever hear any speculation from him on that subject. He'd wanted her to understand that before they reached Fairplay.

Longarm was feeling pretty good now, all things considered. Pretty good indeed.

174

Chapter 42

Longarm was seated in Harry's study, his long legs crossed and a cup of coffee steaming at his elbow. Damn, he was glad to have that coffee. Harry was upstairs with Elaine and Janet. Which was just where he should be, the three of them together. The doctor was up there too. He'd said Janet should already have come out from under the influence of the laudanum, but apparently one never knew about these things. Hopefully there would be a chance for Longarm to see her after she knew Elaine was safe. She still hadn't been able to tell him whatever it was she felt the need to say to him.

Longarm yawned and reached for the coffee cup. It had been one helluva long night. Worthwhile, of course. But long. He was more than ready to catch up on his sleep. Just as soon as he was finished here.

He heard the front door pull, and moments after, the sound of voices in the foyer, the biddy Harry had introduced as Mrs. Whitcomb and a masculine voice. Boots thumped on the hardwood floor and the study door pushed open. "You wanted to see me, Mr. . . ." Ed Kramer stopped short when he saw who was in the study.

"You! I told you to get the hell out of my town."

"I came back," Longarm said. He set the coffee cup down on its saucer, but did not rise to greet the town marshal.

"Then you'd best leave again. That warrant is still good."

"D'you know what a moot point is, Kramer?"

"Of course I do," Kramer blustered, a note of uncertainty in his voice.

"Well, that's what your warrant is. Moot. Which means it don't matter no more."

"How do you figure—"

"The kidnappers are dead, Kramer. Every one of them."

"All three?"

"Four," Longarm corrected.

"I only saw three when I delivered the money this morning."

"Yeah, so I noticed."

"Noticed?"

"I was there, Kramer. I watched you turn over the burro and ride back to town."

"That's right. Just like I told Mr. Faire when I got back here. I didn't have any choice. They said they would release the girl after they counted the money. I told them how much it was, of course. Thirty-two thousand, not the forty they wanted. I explained to them that was all there was. They promised me they'd release the girl. Did they?"

Longarm shook his head. "No, I'm afraid they decided they couldn't let her live for fear she could identify them."

"That's a shame."

"Yes, isn't it," Harry Faire said, coming into the room behind Kramer and slumping into his favorite chair. He looked immeasurably sad for a man whose daughter had just been returned to him. Longarm hadn't thought Harry could be that much of an actor, but then there are some things you can't tell about a man until you see him in action. So to speak. "Tell me something. Ed," the banker said.

"Certainly."

"Why is it that Custis recovered only sixteen thousand at the cabin where the gang was hiding."

"Sixteen?"

"Sixteen in gold," Harry said, "plus the loot from the robbery. That was mostly in currency and silver, very little gold."

Kramer shrugged. "They must have hidden half of the ransom money for some reason. To come back to later or something. It's a shame we can't ask them where it is, isn't it."

"Custis seems to think he knows where it is."

"Maybe he does at that. Maybe he stashed it away for himself. Have you thought about that possibility?"

"I'm sure that did not happen, Ed."

"He wouldn't tell you, Mr. Faire. A man who would steal that much money would sure as hell lie about it after to cover his own tracks."

"Yes, I suspect a thief could be expected to lie at that."

"You probably won't never know what happened to the rest of your money, Mr. Faire. I guess you should count yourself lucky to have got any of it back, don't you think?"

Harry shrugged and turned to look toward the doorway. The light tock-tock of a lady's footsteps could be heard crossing the foyer. Harry turned to look, and so did Kramer, but Longarm's eyes stayed fixed on the Fairplay marshal.

Longarm knew the exact instant that Elaine Faire walked into the room. Ed Kramer's face and neck lost all color as the shock of seeing her made him as pale as a papier-mâché figure.

"Elaine . . . how . . . I thought they said . . ."

"The kidnappers decided to kill her, Ed," Longarm said. "I overheard them saying so. They didn't have time to go through with it."

"I, uh . . . that's wonderful. Simply wonderful. Isn't it."

"Ayuh, it is wonderful indeed," Longarm drawled.

"There is something you may be interested in, Ed," Harry said.

"Yes, sir?"

"Elaine tells me the gang members talked about their boss. Someone who lives in town here, from what she overheard. This boss of theirs planned the robbery and recruited them for the job. The kidnapping was an afterthought, so to speak. One of them, a boy named Willy, apologized to her for it. The others insisted that she die."

"Did these men say who this local man is?" Kramer asked. "If you have even a hint, I'll see Judge Brendan about a warrant."

"They never mentioned his name," Harry said. "A pity, isn't it."

"Yes, it sure is," the marshal agreed.

Harry stood and reached for Elaine's hand. The girl looked better now that she was cleaned up and had proper clothes on. The ordeal had left no visible signs. Longarm was glad for that.

"Would you please excuse us?" Harry asked. "We have . . . arrangements to make. While we were upstairs, our dear Janet roused long enough to see her baby safely home. She gave Elaine a kiss, then closed her eyes and allowed herself an escape from the pain."

"She's gone?" Longarm asked.

Harry nodded.

"I'm sorry, old friend. God, I'm so sorry."

"Thank you, Custis. I know you mean that as deeply in your own way as I do. Would you . . . tend to things here now? I haven't the heart."

"Sure, Harry. I'll do that."

Harry and Elaine left, leaving Longarm and Kramer alone in the lovely room.

"What was that all about?" Kramer snarled.

Longarm smiled at him. "You."

"What the hell are you talking about?"

"It all fits once the pieces are in view, Ed. Hiring that poor drunk to try an' shoot me. That was stupid, Ed. He didn't have a chance. But then arranging murder isn't what Sophie is good at, is it.''

"You've gone out of your mind, Long."

"I don't think so. You were out of town, but you sent a note to Sophie telling her to get me outa the way. I talked to your deputy, by the way. He admits one of the notes he delivered that night was to Sophie. Hell, maybe the search warrant will turn it up. If she's dumb enough to hire a rummy for an ambush, maybe she's dumb enough to hold onto an incriminating note too. We'll see when we go through her papers. Prob'ly we'll find the missing sixteen thousand in her place too. There or at your house. We'll search both."

Kramer's color had yet to return. He looked like he was being repeatedly punched in the stomach.

"It woulda been you that tried to kill me through the hotel window an' shot that poor little girl instead. I owe you for that one, Ed. I figure to collect on the debt."

"You can't prove . . . you're crazy, Long. You have it in for me. Have had for years. Everybody knows that."

"It's true, Ed. I've despised you for years. Now I get t' do something about it."

"Not without proof you can't."

Longarm stood. He smiled. "Oh, I expect we'll find enough proof when we serve those warrants. But just like your warrant, Ed, by then the whole thing will be moot." With his left hand he dragged his coat open so Kramer could get a good look at the battered grips of the big Colt revolver at Longarm's waist. "By then, Ed, you'll be dead."

Kramer shook his head. "No. You can't make me draw against you. I won't do it."

"Ed, I ain't asking you to. We're alone in this room, Ed. It ain't but you and me. And the story that comes out of here is whatever way I want to tell it." Longarm grinned. "If I say you went for your gun, Ed, then that's the way it will be written down."

"My God, Long."

"Sensible," Longarm agreed solemnly. "Talk to Him. After all, you're fixing to meet Him."

Kramer crumpled under the pressure. Frightened, positive that Longarm would kill him regardless, the Fairplay town marshal made a desperate grab for his gun.

The bellow of Longarm's .44 filled the Faire household, punctuating their grief with a measure of justice.

Chapter 43

Three days later, Longarm stood in a Leadville hotel room whipping shaving soap into a lather and brushing it onto his face. That done, he stared toward the mirror before him, his eyes unfocused while he dragged his razor back and forth over a strop to finish honing it.

Behind him he heard the plump, busty redhead stir as she began to waken. She was a nice enough woman, but not what he wanted right this minute.

But then the company he really wanted was no longer available. And never would be.

It still rankled him too that he would never know what it was Janet wanted to say to him. Something so private that she would not even transmit it through Harry. And Longarm would not have thought there was anything she could not have shared with Harry.

Not that there was any sense in worrying about it. He would never know.

He feathered the edge of the razor against the ball of his

thumb, and was satisfied with the barely discernible *ping* of metal that resulted.

Pulling at his neck to smooth the skin, he leaned closer to the mirror and laid the edge lightly onto his cheek beneath his left eye.

For an instant Longarm found himself staring into his own eye in the mirror as if he had never seen it before.

And for that instant he thought . . . no. Hell, no. He was imagining things. He was as loco as the late Ed Kramer had claimed if for one instant he believed that was why Elaine Faire had looked so almighty familiar to him. Or why Elaine's mother had wanted to speak to him in private.

It was coincidence, nothing more than coincidence, that Harry and Janet's girl had eyes the same color as Longarm's.

Her posture, her bones . . . no, that was pure imagination. The girl didn't look anything like him. She couldn't.

Why, she was . . . he thought back. Counted the years. Counted months too. He shook his head.

No, dammit. He could prove it. Just ask her birth date. That would prove it.

Longarm grunted. He was not, absolutely was *not* going to demean himself by asking a stupid question like that. No way.

He grunted again, and picked up a towel to wipe the lather off his face. He would stop at a barbershop later for his shave. He felt a mite shaky this morning, and didn't especially want to slice a cheek open. Not that there was any reason. He was feeling just fine. Really. No reason he should be shaking. No reason whatsoever.

"Lover."

He looked at her in the reflection before him. "Yeah honey."

"Come give me some more of your sugar, lover."

"Sugar, sweetheart?" He wished he could remember her name. Maybe it would come to him later.

The redhead smiled. "When it's as sweet as yours, lover, I call it sugar."

Longarm smiled and folded the razor closed. Hell, he

didn't have time to shave right now anyway.

And as for that other thought, about Elaine and why she'd seemed so familiar, well, that was all in his head. There wasn't a damn thing to it.

He tossed the towel aside and headed for the bed, an erection already beginning to bump and throb as the redhead opened her arms to receive him.

Watch for

LONGARM AND THE REBEL EXECUTIONER

227th novel in the exciting LONGARM series
from Jove

Coming in November!